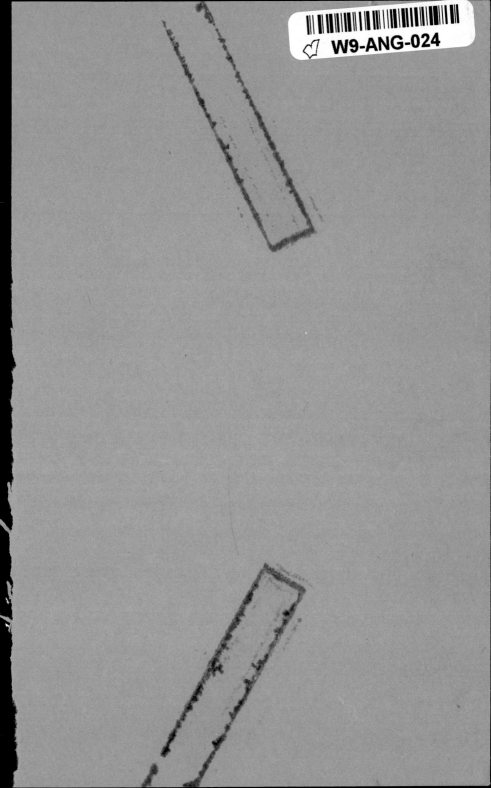

BOOKS BY BARBARA CORCORAN

Axe-Time, Sword-Time
Cabin in the Sky
A Dance to Still Music
The Long Journey
Meet Me at Tamerlaine's Tomb
A Row of Tigers
Sasha, My Friend
A Trick of Light
The Winds of Time
All the Summer Voices
The Clown
Don't Slam the Door When You Go
Sam
This Is a Recording
The Faraway Island

Make no sound

BARBARA CORCORAN

Make no sound

ATHENEUM 1977 NEW YORK

LIBRARY OF CONGRESS CATALOGING IN PUBLICATION DATA

Corcoran, Barbara. Make no sound.

SUMMARY: A twelve-year-old girl living in Hawaii gets caught up
in the myths and superstitions of the area.
[1. Hawaii—Fiction] I. Title.
PZ7.C814Mak   [Fic]   77–2001
ISBN 0–689–30580–X

Published simultaneously in Canada by McClelland & Stewart, Ltd.
Manufactured in the United States of America by
The Book Press, Brattleboro, Vermont
Designed by Mary M. Ahern
First Edition

To the BC Club,
Keaau School,
Hawaii

Make no sound

1

MELODY ducked away from her mother's hand. "What did I do now?" she muttered, but she didn't listen to her mother's stream of complaint. A teacher she had had once said that punishment was a child's chance to learn from experience, but that teacher didn't know Melody's mother. There was no rhyme nor reason to her mother's punishments. The same thing that brought a slap one day might bring approval the next, or, more often, indifference.

The best defense was to make herself as nearly invisible as possible, make her mother forget she was there. No matter how mad or rebellious she felt, just sit tight. Some day she'd be old enough to disappear for real.

Today her mother was jumpy because she was making plans. That always made her edgy. She sat on one of the twin beds in the hotel room, with her feet on the frame of the cot that was shoved between the beds. Fanned all around her were brochures and maps and the yellow pads of paper that she made lists on. She kept saying, as if it were Melody's fault, that she had to decide right away where they were going to live on this island, because the hotel was too expensive to hang around in.

Melody went out on the lanai to get out of the way and to look at this new place. Hilo, Hawaii. The Big Island, the Orchid Island, the Volcano Island, the Rainbow Island. She liked the way it looked. There were flowers everywhere. San Diego had flowers too, but this place was like a flowering jungle, with blossoms all over the trees and bushes as well as down where you expected them to be.

The park behind the hotel looked like a picture of Japan, with pagodas and carved stone gods and little arched bridges.

And off in the distance were the volcanoes. Farthest off, with snow on top of it, was Mauna Kea, "dormant but not extinct," the brochure said. Nearer were Mauna Loa and Kilauea, "active." She shivered with an almost-pleasant little fear. A couple of years ago she had read "The Last Days of Pompeii" and been scared. But maybe these volcanoes were different, because here were all these people living here. They wouldn't do that if they were about to be swallowed up by fiery lava, would they?

Maybe they were like her mother, though. Her mother could almost always deny the existence of anything she didn't want to believe in. She refused to believe that Southern California might have a big earthquake, just because there had never been one in her lifetime, and she'd grown up in Orange County, hadn't she, so she ought to know, shouldn't she? That's what she said. Anyway she didn't believe in science.

Melody looked down at the swimming pool and saw her two brothers. Brian as usual was showing off. He teetered up and down on the end of the diving board, laughing and talking in his loud way, for the benefit of three girls who were watching him.

They think he's terrific, Melody thought. Big, handsome, tanned, super swimmer, charm all over the place. They ought to have him for a brother. She laughed as he lost his balance and hit the water with arms and legs flailing. But he'd pretend he'd done it on purpose, and they'd think he was a great comedian. Brian always came out ahead.

George lay flat on his back on the cement surround, his hat over his eyes. Not even a towel under him. Suffering. George suffered a lot lately. He was naturally quiet and withdrawn, but since his sixteenth birthday he had moved into some little world of his own. He hardly talked to anyone, and especially to Melody. She didn't know what his problem was, and she wasn't all that interested. He had never paid much attention to her anyway, except the time she cut her knee and he took charge and got her to a doctor. Anyway he never punched her or tripped her up or tried to get her into trouble the way Brian did. Mean, *mean*, Brian was.

Her mother called to her impatiently, and she went inside.

"What are you doing?"

"Just looking at the fish."

"What fish?"

"There's big enormous goldfish in that little stream below us."

Her mother went out and looked. "Carp. They're Japanese carp." She glanced at Melody with a flicker of annoyance. "It stands to reason they aren't goldfish. They aren't gold."

"Oh," Melody said.

"Can't you see they couldn't be goldfish? Goldfish are small. And gold. Look at them. They're pink and red and all kinds of colors. You must learn to observe." She went into the room, smoothing down her new pink pantsuit. "I want to explain to you about our situation. Sit down."

That meant she was at the stage in her planning where she needed to say it all out loud. Melody was the listener. But she had learned to look as if she were listening when she wasn't. This time she did listen, because she wanted to know what they were going to do here. Her mother had made Hawaii sound like paradise, and it did look like paradise, but Melody knew from experience that paradises turned real sooner or later, and had to be coped with.

"I've been talking to some real estate people downstairs," her mother said. "Rents here are outrageous. Though not as bad as Honolulu. And there aren't all that many places for rent anyway. But this woman I talked to, she's going to call me back . . ." She looked at her watch. "Her boss has just bought a small apartment house over on the leeward side."

Melody stopped listening to think about the word "leeward." Her mother always picked up local language right away. If there was a leeward side, this must be windward.

". . . a manager," her mother was saying. "I told her about that motel I managed in Carlsbad. The apartment is too small for you children, but I can find a little house . . ." She wasn't really talking to Melody; she was talking to the unseen audience that was always with her. Sometimes Melody pictured that audience as her mother's four former husbands: the first mysterious one who was never mentioned; Jim, who was Brian's father and who had beat up on his wife and child; Harry, who was George's father and had run away with a bartender's wife; and Melody's own father, Peter, who left them because he got sick of being prayed over. He had happened to come along during her mother's religious phase. Right now she was down on all churches. She still prayed over her children a lot, and had long, one-sided conversations with God, in which she told him her plans and hopes and complaints, gave him advice, and criticized politicians. She also spoke to him often about flying saucers, which she believed in and referred to as God's little boats.

". . . and that would solve the whole thing," she was saying.

Melody wondered if she could go outside without her mother's noticing. She stood up carefully, but her mother fixed her with a hard stare. Melody stood still, but in her mind she left the scene. She had practiced doing this so often, she could turn her mind into another channel altogether. Sometimes, though, her mother knew she was doing that.

"Melody," she said sharply, "you're not listening."

"Sure I am. You said you could find us a place . . ."

"I said that at least three minutes ago. Your mind will curl up and rot if you shut it off like that."

"Will it really?" Melody tried to picture a curled-up mind.

"If I indulged myself the way you children do, where would we be, I'd like to know? Up a creek, that's where. I have to shoulder all the burden. I get no help from any of you. None. In spite of my health, I have to do it all." She often referred to her health with loving sadness, although as far as Melody could see, it was excellent.

"Can I go down to the pool now?" she asked

8

"No, you cannot. I have to go out. If that woman calls, tell her I'll be back in thirty minutes. Three-o minutes, Melody. I have to see some people." She leaned toward the mirror, combing out her blonde hair and improving on her lipstick.

"You look nice," Melody said. Her mother really was pretty.

Their eyes met in the mirror. "Be sure you get that woman's number so I can call her back." She put on the pink cardigan with the tiny pearls stitched across the shoulders. "When the boys come in, tell them not to drip all over the rug. I'm not about to be charged for a new rug."

Melody could imagine Brian's reaction if she told him that. He'd wring out his wet trunks on the floor, just to be ornery. That was Brian all over. George would never drip on the rug. George was very neat. And he avoided doing things that he might be yelled at about.

When her mother had gone, Melody flopped on the bed. It had been a long, long day, and she was sleepy. She tried to stay awake, because she was sure the boys wouldn't have thought to take a key, and Brian would rage if she didn't hear him and let him in immediately. On the railing of the lanai a speckled dove cooed. She had to keep pinching herself to stay awake.

2

RIAN drove the rented Pinto up the Hamakua coast. The car was crowded, with the four of them and all the luggage. Melody was squashed into a corner of the back seat, a suitcase between her and George, and a canvas bag under her feet. She had lent George her radio, and he had the earplug in his ear, listening with the dreamy expression people get when they're listening to something no one else can hear.

She loved that radio. Her father had bought it for her just before they left California. He used to send her money, until he found out that her mother kept it. "House expenses," her mother always said. "I can't raise three children on scratch feed." But all three husbands paid child support. Melody didn't know about the others, but her father paid two hundred dollars a month. Still her mother said she had to slave night and day to keep a roof over their heads. It was because she had lost her last job as hostess in an elegant restaurant that they had come to Hawaii. "To a better, fuller life," she said. Every move they had ever made had been to achieve a better, fuller life. Melody's dad, who hadn't wanted her to go, had said, "Your mother is always chasing rainbows." Melody thought it was funny when she found out that this was called the Rainbow Island. She thought of it again as they passed a sign pointing to Rainbow Falls.

Brian always drove so fast, you couldn't see anything. As a big truck loaded down with some kind of produce roared past them scarily close, Brian swore. "Road hog," he shouted into the wind.

"Don't drive so fast," his mother said. She was reading a magazine that told all about what Liz Taylor and Jackie Onassis were up to, and why Troubled Nurse left her intern husband when she found him in the midst of a sex orgy in the hospital linen room.

Brian waved a hand toward the fields. "What is all that stuff anyway? All these trucks are loaded with it. What is it, Edith?" He and George always called their mother "Edith." Melody never did. She always thought of her as Her.

"Sugar cane," his mother said.

"Sugar comes from beets, Edith."

Without looking up from her reading, his mother said, "And from sugar cane, Mr. Smarty." They were sarcastic with each other, but he was her favorite.

"My mother, the book of knowledge," Brian said.

Melody wished he would slow down so she could

see more. She caught quick glimpses of huge water-falls pouring down over the rocks, but they were gone as soon as she saw them. Far down, at the base of the cliff they were driving along, the sea sparkled. Sometimes they drove over long-legged bridges that spanned deep chasms.

A quick rain shower caught them, with the sun still out, and Brian turned on the windshield wipers, cussing.

"Mind your language, Mr. Dirty Mouth," his mother said.

"Oh, come off it, Edith." He looked in the rear-view mirror. "Can't you make those creeps in the back move that suitcase? I can't see."

"Move the suitcase," their mother said.

"There's no place to move it." Melody tried to scrunch up tighter in the corner.

"Helpful as usual," Brian said.

Oh, shut up, she said in her mind—shut up, shut up, shut your mean mouth.

An old car rattled past them with a bumper sticker that said DON' LAUGH MY CAR.

"What language do Hawaiians speak?" Melody said.

"That's a brilliant question," Brian said. "English speak English, don't they, and Italians speak Italian. Hawaiians speak Hawaiian. Surprise, surprise."

"I didn't ask you," she said.

"As a matter of fact, they don't," her mother said. "They speak a kind of garbled English called Pidgin. They throw in Hawaiian words, though, like 'mahalo,' 'kane,' and 'wahine.' "

"What do they mean?"

" 'Mahalo' is a word I'm afraid my children will seldom use. It means thank you. 'Kane' means man, 'wahine' is woman."

Melody wondered if she would understand people when she went to school.

Her mother took off her glasses and folded the magazine. "Filth," she said. "Nothing but shame and vice and sin abroad in the world."

"Nobody makes you read it," Brian said. "You love it."

"A person has to know what exists in order to fight it." She was in a good mood because she had gotten the job of managing the apartment house in wherever it was they were going.

"Are we keeping this car?" Brian asked.

"Are you out of your mind? At sixteen dollars a day plus mileage? No way."

"We have to have a car."

"Then get out and earn the money, Mr. Big Shot."

He flared up. "I might. I just might, you know. I'm sick of school. I've had it right up to here."

"So leave. I'd be delighted. One less mouth to feed."

He grumbled, but Melody knew he wouldn't leave school till he had to, because he'd rather put up with school than work.

The rain was like a heavy mist, something like a San Diego fog. She curled up in her mind and tried to imagine herself a pink Japanese carp. She used to imagine herself a butterfly until she read about some kind of butterfly that has no digestive system. It just gets born and starves to death. It seemed careless of God to have overlooked a thing like a butterfly's digestive system.

Her mother twisted around in her seat and gave them a bored look. She hated to just sit, but Brian made such a fuss if she didn't let him drive. "You two back there, cat got your tongue?"

George removed the earplug. "What?"

"It's like riding with a pair of zombies. Never a word out of you."

George put the earplug back.

Melody tried to think of something to say. "Some butterflies don't have any digestive system."

Her mother looked interested for a moment. She liked random information. She always read the fillers in the newspapers and often quoted them. Things like: "Utah became the forty-fifth state on January 4, 1896." Or: "Squid sometimes appear to fly because they skim the sea with their side fins." She considered the butterfly problem and said, "I don't believe it."

"I read it. That's why they die so soon. They use

up their energy and just crumble away." Melody felt sad for the poor butterflies.

"That would be inefficient and wasteful, and the Creator of all things great and small is never inefficient or wasteful."

"No?" Brian said. "What about dinosaurs?"

"If we had the wisdom to know, we'd see that dinosaurs had some place in the scheme of things."

"Bull," Brian said.

"You watch your tongue, young man."

"The conversation in this family is enough to make you throw up."

"And what is your contribution, Mr. Genius?"

Brian speeded up for a sharp curve and the car skidded.

"Watch it! You do that again and you can walk the rest of the way."

"I'll give you an interesting fact," he said with a grin. "You like facts so much. There's pot growing all over this island. They say Kona gold is a real trip."

"You can just forget that kind of talk."

"It's not talk—it's for real."

"You know what you'll get if you ever monkey with that stuff again."

He laughed. "What, Edith? A lickin'? I'm bigger than you are now."

Melody craned her neck to watch the great arc of a rainbow, till the car cut around a curve and lost it.

After a while her mother said to Brian, "Turn off

here for a minute. We'll get a cup of coffee or something."

Brian grinned, but he turned off, driving fast down the narrow road that said HONOKAA, SPEED 25 MPH. Some chickens squawked and scattered out of his way, and a boy on a bicycle swerved and almost hit the ditch.

"Are you mad?" his mother said. "Slow down before we get a ticket." She hit his knee with her fist.

He cut into a small parking lot where there was a sandwich place, and stopped so suddenly that the suitcase slid off the seat and hit the front seat.

George took out his earplug. "Are we there?"

"Sure," Brian said. "How do you like it?"

"If you'd take that stupid thing out of your ear," his mother said, "you'd know what's going on. We are stopping for refreshment."

"Gin break," Brian said, and laughed when his mother gave him a venomous look.

Melody had to struggle to get out of the back seat, but it felt good to stretch. She saw her mother disappear with her large straw bag in the direction of the ladies' room. She would come back smelling of gin. For years she had kept a mixture of tea and gin in a thermos jug, sipping on it all day. "I get so dry," she would say. "I just get so dry, I have to have a little liquid for my poor throat." She still kept the thermos handy, but more and more often she would disappear into her bedroom or the bathroom and come back reeking of gin.

One day Brian said, "She's taking straight shots now."

Melody found the bottles in the trash. Sometimes Brian caught his mother at it—he lay in wait for it—but if he spoke of it, she would say, "I don't know what you are referring to. I take a little spirits on the doctor's orders. You know very well about my heart."

Once when she had said that, Brian had laughed so hard, she threw a Disneyland figurine at him and it broke. It was Donald Duck.

Brian got out of the car and pushed Melody up against one of the small iron tables. "Stupid idiot," he said. He had several voices. This one was his mean voice, pitched low so other people wouldn't hear him. His charm voice was loud and cheerful. When he talked to girls, he used his sexy voice, and with his mother his voice was hard and scornful.

"Off in a fog," he said to Melody. "Spaced out."

Her mother called it daydreaming, and it irritated her, too. Melody's friend Marg had said it was Melody's special quality. "You can switch your mind around, Mel," she had said. "What I think is, I think you're an enchanted person. I'll bet if you work on it, you could slip all around in different time zones and places."

Melody thought of that conversation now. She and

Marg had been lying on the sand at Capistrano Beach. "Maybe," she had said, "I could get so I choose my own time and place." The idea had fascinated her ever since. Maybe she was really a changeling, a person from another century or even another planet, caught in this time warp. She tried to think what time she felt at home in. Maybe the Druids. Or the Vikings. She'd ride in the Viking boats, the only girl, and she'd hang flowers around their necks when they had a victory.

Her mother came back and ordered coffee for herself and milk shakes for her children. "Hurry up," she said. "I've got work to do before night falls." She always said "before night falls," and when Melody was little, she had been frightened by that night that might come crashing down on her.

She sucked on her straw till it gurgled. She would have liked to go to the bathroom but the others were piling into the car and yelling at her to hurry up.

Brian made one of his spectacular U-turns. Their mother said this was the second biggest city on the island, but it looked more like a little country town.

As they passed a group of dark-skinned Hawaiians, Brian said in his tough voice, "Ain't they got any white people over here?"

"Stop saying 'ain't,' " his mother said.

A pickup truck came rattling up a steep hill, almost hidden by the tall sugar cane, and cut in front of Brian, who leaned on his horn. The big Hawaiian, with a straw hat shoved back on his head, looked back, grinned and held up one hand, fist clenched and thumb and little finger raised.

Brian gunned the engine and bore down on the pickup.

"What are you doing?" his mother shrieked at him.

"He threw me a dirty finger. I'm gonna get him."

"Cool it," George said. "That's a friendly gesture, stupid."

Brian turned his rage toward George. "Who you calling stupid?"

"How do you know it's friendly?" their mother said to George.

"I listen. I look. I don't spend my time showing off for a bunch of girls." As Brian passed the truck, George leaned forward and made the same gesture toward the driver. "Shah-ka," he called.

The man's big voice shouted, "Shah-ka, bruddah."

Melody turned and waved, and the man waved back, grinning broadly.

"What does that word mean?" she asked George.

But he had already put the radio plug in his ear, and he only looked at her blankly.

"Some people know so much," Brian said. "Some people are such wise guys."

"Save your breath," his mother said. "He can't hear you."

3

ELODY sat up. She had fallen asleep, and now they were in an altogether different kind of country, high and arid, with pines and cactus. They passed cattle ranches and horses grazing in pastureland. She had never thought of Hawaii as looking like this.

They stopped at a town and had hot dogs in a shopping center. There were a lot of things to see, including a cowboy museum that George wanted to go into, but their mother said it cost too much. She bought a pamphlet about the Parker Ranch to read to them instead, and George had to be content with touching the big saddles in the leather shop.

When they were on the road again, their mother read them snatches from the pamphlet. This part of the island had been overrun with wild cattle, and a man named Parker had been hired to take care of the problem. He brought in cowboys from South America, called paniolos.

"Isn't that interesting," she said. "This is the biggest . . . now listen to this . . . the Parker ranch is the biggest privately owned cattle ranch in the U.S.A."

"Bull," Brian said.

"It says so right here in black and white."

They were on a road high above the ocean, and the landscape turned into acres of black broken lava remains, so frightening-looking that Melody wondered for a moment if her magic powers had put her down on another planet. The ground looked as if it would cut you to pieces if you stepped on it. Even George had shut off the radio and was staring at it. She heard him say, "Wow!" under his breath.

"It's an old lava flow from Mauna Kea," their mother said, reading from the pamphlet again. "Biggest volcano in the world. And out there . . ." She pointed dramatically to the ocean. ". . . are a line of mountains more than two miles high that are still below the surface of the sea. Think of that!"

"Are you telling me . . ." Brian began in his argumentative voice.

"I am telling you facts, Mr. Know-It-All, facts. Straight from the Hawaii Volcanoes National Park authorities."

Melody looked at the calm blue-green sea, trying to imagine the mountains. What if her Viking ship crashed into one of those invisible mountains? They'd all be goners.

21

". . . fountains of melted rock," her mother was reading, "shoot into the air, and the lava flows in a stream that's two thousand degrees Fahrenheit. Now that's hot, children."

For once Melody was glad Brian was driving fast. The place scared her.

"Here's the part about Madam Pele," her mother said.

Brian laughed. "You mean they got a madam doing business in this godforsaken place?"

"Don't be crude. Madam Pele is the goddess of the volcano."

"This island is full of crazies," Brian said disgustedly. "Goddess of the volcano!"

His mother ignored him. "She was a pale-skinned stranger who came here long ago. She lives in the crater of Kilauea. She dug the crater with her magic stick."

Melody leaned forward to hear above Brian's mocking laughter.

"Whenever she appears, there's a volcanic eruption. If she appears on the street, don't touch her or your hand will be burned."

"What does this chick look like?" Brian said.

"Sometimes she's an old white-haired woman, sometimes she's young and beautiful. She always carries her magic stick."

"We've moved into one big nut house," Brian said.

22

"This island is a nut house. Hey, if I run across this Pele babe, I'll take her out in an outrigger, and the island won't have anything to worry about."

"I might have to worry about you," his mother said.

"Oh, this kid can handle goddesses. Every time."

"What if she's in her old woman get-up?" George said.

"I'll wait. I never saw the chick yet I couldn't out-wait."

"You're disgusting," his mother said, but she didn't mean it. She believed that Brian was irresistible.

Melody was thinking about that magic stick. It would have to be really powerful to dig in that hard black rock. Maybe she would get herself a stick. How did you make it magic, though?

"Where did she get her magic stick?" she said.

"Woolworth's—where'd you think?" Brian said.

Melody touched her mother's shoulder to get her attention, and her mother jumped.

"Don't do that, Melody."

"I'm sorry." She wanted to ask if it burned, but they would only laugh. "How did the stick get to be magic? Did she say a spell or what?"

"Melody, you ask the weirdest questions." She looked out the window, thinking. "I suppose if she was magic, her stick would automatically be magic."

23

"My God," Brian said, "you sound as if you believe it."

"Of course I don't. It's just local superstition." Then she added in a voice so low Melody hardly heard her, "But you never know, do you."

4

HE TOWN wasn't a real town at all. It was a tiny fishing village hung on the edge of the sea, with a few new houses, the small apartment house, and fishermen's shacks. There were no stores or schools, not even a gas station. Big trees with red blossoms lined the only street, and side lanes went down to the water. There was no real beach.

The ground was black lava, but things had grown in it, a thick tangle of trees and bushes that looked like movies of jungles Melody had seen in school. It was hard to believe all this had grown from the hard rock. Melody picked up a handful of loose pebbles. Madam Pele's potting soil, she thought, and smiled at the notion. Mr. Burstein would like that if she put it in a theme. He'd write "Good!" in the margin. She was going to miss Mr. Burstein. And Marg. And the other kids. She'd gone to that school three years, which was a long time for her.

Her mother had bossed the unloading of the car and then sent Brian with it to Kona to turn it in. He was supposed to hitch a ride back. "Don't get into any fights," she told him.

Melody and George had been told to get lost while their mother settled in. George had disappeared at once. Melody walked down to a boat landing and sat down on the edge of the launching platform. No one was around except a man some distance out in knee-deep water, fishing. He wore a faded blue cotton jacket and a cone-shaped hat, like a fisherman in a Japanese print.

Melody had almost always lived near the ocean, but being on a small island right in the middle of it was different. It gave her a queasy feeling. She could almost feel the rise and fall of the tides.

She didn't know what to do with herself. She had walked the length of the street and looked at the new houses and at the fishermen's houses built on stilts close to the water. They interested her. Some of them had latticework around the lower part, with clothes hanging from poles. Maybe they didn't have closets.

She had looked at the tiny white steepled church at the end of the street, and peeked inside at the cool, dark interior. The church looked as if it were made of adobe, although that didn't seem possible here. She couldn't tell the denomination because the name of the church was some long string of Hawaiian words with all those vowels. Her mother said they had only twelve letters in their alphabet. That seemed strange. She had always thought the alphabet was everybody's alphabet.

Away from the waterfront the air was warm, but there was a breeze off the sea. A slight rustle behind her made her turn around. A strange-looking animal was peering at her with bright, curious eyes. He was long and thin like a weasel, with a tapering head, very short legs, and a long bushy tail. He looked a little like a mink, but not really.

"Who are you?" she said.

He didn't seem afraid of her until she made a move to get up, then he loped off into the brush. She peered into the tangle but couldn't see him, so she found a weathered limb, stripped off the leaves, and poked at the brush, but he was gone.

A pickup pulling a boat trailer with a boat on it was backing in. A big young man with a mass of reddish frizzed-out hair like an Afro jumped down from the cab. He grinned at her, his teeth very white in his brown face.

"Aloha," he said.

She was surprised. It hadn't occurred to her that people really said "aloha," like "hi." She had thought it was more like a slogan.

He jumped up and down on the launching ramp a couple of times, and called out something she didn't understand. Another young Hawaiian got out of the pickup and glanced at Melody, but he didn't speak.

The tall one said, "Eh, man, le's go."

She moved back to a safe distance and watched them unload the boat. They did a lot of shouting and heaving and groaning, with sharp yells of warning as if disaster were about to strike. But at last they had the small fishing boat on the ramp.

The second man got back into the pickup, but the tall one came over to Melody. She took a step backward, but he certainly looked friendly.

"Who you? Haole?"

"I don't know," she said.

He threw back his head and laughed. "You don' know. She don' know who she is."

"I'm Melody Baxter," she said, a little annoyed. "I know who I am. I don't know that word you said. Howlie?"

"You new here, right? Stranger here?"

"Yes."

"A haole, dat's a stranger. White like you. Not brown like me." He slapped his bare chest. "Eh, we gotta leave dat boat a lil while. You watch him for us, okay? Scare off bad guys with your big stick, yeah?"

She had forgotten she still had the stick.

"All dem people." He waved vaguely into the air. "Mo' bettah dey leave our boat alone. Someday I give you ride in da boat, yeah?"

The other man yelled at him.

"Right, right, I come." He smiled at Melody. "We be back quick-quick. Aloha."

"Aloha," she said. And as he turned away, she held up her hand in a fist, with thumb and little finger up. "Shah-ka." She gave the gesture a little extra flourish by waving her stick with the other hand.

He burst out laughing. "Shah-ka, sistah. You learn quick."

"Moku," the man in the pickup shouted impatiently.

Moku yelled back. "I spik you later. Now I spik dis lil malihini." And to Melody he said, "What your name?"

"Melody Baxter." She added, "I've got two brothers." She always said that so people would think she had good protection.

"Bruddahs? Two mo' Baxters, yeah?"

"No, one is a Miller and one is a Gould." As he looked puzzled, she added, "They're my half-brothers."

"You goin' live around here?"

"My mother is managing the apartment house."

"Ohhh, I see. Yeah, okay. I see you later."

The man in the pickup leaned on the horn, and Moku ran to the driver's side. "We be back bumbye." He revved the engine, and the pickup skidded forward, tires throwing up a spray of crumbled lava.

"Well," Melody said aloud. She went closer to the boat. The name on the bow was NANILEI, in letters badly faded. She touched the bow with her stick. " 'Nanilei,' I shall protect you with my magic stick." She examined the stick critically. It wasn't really magic yet, of course. She wished she knew if Madam Pele said spells over hers, and what they were. Probably a Hawaiian-language spell. Maybe she could ask Moku when she got to know him better. He seemed nice.

She watched a bird fly low over the water. He was white with black wing patches, a yellow bill, and a long white tail that forked at the end. As she watched, he dived into the water and came up with a fish. He'd got his supper. Poor fish.

She leaned down and stared into the clear water. All kinds of fish darted around. She took off her sneakers. The water felt very warm, and the coarse black gravel was rough under her toes.

She walked out a little way. Something shot past her foot, something very long and snakelike. Quickly she retreated. She had read that there were no snakes in the Islands, but maybe that meant just on land. This was going to be an interesting place all right, but it might turn out scary in ways she hadn't thought of.

5

$\mathcal{M}$OKU didn't come back. Melody waited about half an hour, then said a couple of spells over the "Nanilei," waved her stick three times over the bow, and left because she was hungry.

Her mother was in the kitchenette reading a newspaper, and George was eating a tuna fish sandwich.

"Where have you been?" her mother said, without waiting for an answer. "Fix yourself a sandwich, if George has left any tuna."

George pushed the can toward Melody. "She rented us a house. Wait till you see it."

Melody tried to read his face. The fact that he had spoken of the house at all meant something, but she couldn't tell whether it was good or bad or just weird.

"It's a sweet little fisherman's cabin," her mother said. "You're going to love it. You can hear the surf pounding right outside your window."

Melody wasn't sure she wanted to hear the surf pounding.

"The man who cleans the pool here told me about it. It belongs to his brother. We were in luck."

Melody looked at George. "What's it like?"

He shrugged and filled his milk glass.

"It's really Hawaiian," her mother said. "The real thing. Very picturesque."

Melody felt uneasy. Sometimes their mother found very odd places to live and thought they were picturesque. Like that abandoned prospector's shack near Palm Desert, the winter after Melody's father left them. That had been picturesque, all right. Four weathered walls and a roof, windows with the glass broken out, and snakes.

"I'll bet you didn't know," her mother said, looking at the paper, "that the very first gasoline-powered automobile in this country was a Duryea, built in 1893 in Springfield, Massachusetts. Way back then. Isn't that something?"

"Is there anything else to eat?" George asked.

"No. I'll go shopping tomorrow."

"There aren't any stores," Melody said.

"I'll have to go to Kona."

"You haven't got a car," George said.

"Oh yes, I have, Mr. Smarty. I have the use of the station wagon that belongs to the owner. What do you think of that?"

George said, "Is it a Duryea?"

Melody laughed. George was funny when he wanted to be. She wished he wanted to be more often.

"It's a nice little Toyota. And you boys are not to touch it."

"Tell Brian, don't tell me."

She looked at her watch. "I wonder where Brian is? He ought to be back."

"Not if there's any action in Kona."

"George, take Melody over to your new home. Take all your junk with you, Melody. It's by the door. Take it *all*, if you please. I haven't got room for a single thing."

Melody collected her duffle bag, her radio, the canvas bag with her writing tablets and the felt-tipped pens, and the two stuffed animals she'd been allowed to bring out of her big collection. One of them was Louella, a bright blue bear with crossed eyes, and the other was Bison, a silky long-haired white buffalo that her father had sent her once from Montana. Louella comforted her, and Bison protected her, with his fierce expression and his shaggy arched head. She knew it was supposed to be stupid to have stuffed animals at her age, but she didn't care. Marg still took an old Raggedy Ann to bed.

George took the duffle bag from her, and they walked up the narrow street. She wanted to ask him more about the house, but she knew what he'd say: "Wait and see."

A short way past the turn-off to the boat launch, he turned down another lane that was bordered on both sides by huge trees with red blossoms like tulips.

George stopped, and for a moment Melody didn't see the cabin, it was so hidden by bushes. Then she saw it—an unpainted weathered little house with a tin roof. It stood on a tall platform, the lower part open to the jungle on two sides, protected on the other sides by broken latticework. Steep rickety steps led to the first floor. The door stood open.

"That's it?" she said.

"That's it."

"Is it . . . safe?" It looked as if it might fall down.

"Safe from what?" George went up the steps. A lizard skittered out of the way.

Melody followed her brother. The house smelled of mildew and mold, but it had recently been swept. There was a room with a small stove and a chipped sink at one end, straw mats on the floor, a wicker chair with sagging bottom, a couch, a plain wooden table and two chairs, one of them with only three legs.

A beaded curtain separated the main room from a tiny bedroom that held a narrow cot, a small chest of drawers marked with cigarette burns, and a small warped mirror.

"That's your room," George said. "Welcome to Paradise."

Out the window, which was almost covered by vines and bushes, she caught a glimpse of the sea, very near.

"Where are you guys going to sleep?"

"Out here. On sleeping bags."

Melody sat on the cot and the springs sagged. "This is the worst yet."

George didn't answer. In a minute she realized that he had gone. She began to unpack. With Bison and Louella sitting on the bed, and her radio on, she felt a little better. She set up the snapshot of her father on the chest of drawers, and tacked to the wall the water color of Balboa marina that her friend Jim had painted. She couldn't hang up her clothes because there was no closet and no hangers. She remembered seeing clothes hung on poles under the house at other fishing shacks.

"Well," she said to Louella and Bison, "it might turn out to be fun, who knows. We'll find out how Hawaiians really live. Not like Waikiki Beach. And at least it's warm." That place in the desert had been cold at night.

She took her magic stick and went out to explore. The tangle of jungle growth was so thick, she had to stay on the path. It led to a small inlet that had crumbled lava instead of sand for a beach. The tide was coming in. The thin white water curling around the black rocks looked as if it would cover the beach at high tide. She poked at a crab with her stick, and he scuttled away.

A gray blob of something attached to a rock rose and fell gently with the tide as if it were alive. Maybe it was. On either side of the path just behind her grew some kind of tree with leaves big enough to wrap around herself like a blanket.

A dark hawk with yellow feet sailed low over the water and headed inland out of her sight. A few minutes later he appeared again with something held in his talons. She shaded her eyes to see. Whatever it was had a very long tail. A rat? She shivered and turned back to the cabin.

Her mother was there with sleeping bags and blankets. She was in a good mood. "Hello-ello. How do you like your new home? Isn't it charming? Oh, you're going to love it. Listen to that sea."

"There isn't any bathroom," Melody said.

"Of course there is. Look through your bedroom window. What do you see?"

"Leaves."

"Look, silly. Right there through the trees. What is that, pray tell?"

Melody followed the direction of her mother's finger and saw an outhouse almost obscured by jungle growth. "That's the bathroom?"

"Certainly. This isn't San Diego, you know. Nothing fake and plastic here."

Melody thought, But *you* have a real bathroom,

but she knew better than to say it. "How do we take a shower?"

"With the whole Pacific Ocean out there, you ask how you take a shower."

"There's a sign down there that says DANGER."

"They just mean exercise due caution. You don't have to swim to Maui to take a bath, you know." She went back to the main room. "Anyway you have running water here, and I brought washcloths."

Melody remembered her English teacher saying the British called a washcloth a "face flannel," and she giggled.

"That's right," her mother said. "Just hadn't used your little old noodle, had you. You're going to have to learn to be resourceful in this world." She was unpacking paper plates. "The place is spotless, I hope you noticed. Clean as a whistle."

"Yes, I noticed."

"Mr. Pepper Wong cleaned it himself. It's his brother's place. We really lucked out."

"I think there are rats out there," Melody said.

"No, it says in the brochure they imported the mongooses to take care of the rats."

"They don't get them all."

Her mother said, "Why do you have to argue about everything?"

Melody felt the surge of frustration that sometimes nearly suffocated her when she had to deal with her mother. Forgetting her resolution to hold her tongue, she said, "Because I saw one. Hanging out of a hawk's mouth."

Her mother hit her a stinging slap on the cheek. "On top of everything else you think you can lie to me."

Melody stepped back, her hand to her face. "It's not a lie. I saw it."

Her mother's face reddened, and Melody backed out of reach. "Hawks don't have rats hanging out of their mouths, you stupid girl."

"This one did." Melody knew she ought to be quiet, let it go, but sometimes she just couldn't. "He flew up out of the jungle near the shack."

"Don't say shack!" her mother yelled. "This is your home. This is Mr. Charlie Wong's house. It is not a shack."

Melody gave up. What could you do when people didn't even stick to the subject? "I'll see you later," she said. She heard her mother still scolding as she went down the lane.

Melody walked along the road in the dappled sunlight of late afternoon. A boy on a motorcycle roared past her, making her cough from the dust.

A big Hawaiian woman sitting on the porch of her little house smiled at her. "Mo' bettah dem kids walk on dere own two feets, not fuss up all dat noise and dust."

Melody smiled, not knowing what to say.

"You b'long lady over to da apartments?"

"Yes. That's my mother."

The woman nodded. "You live by Wong's house."

"Yes."

"Don' you go swim dat water."

"Is it dangerous?"

"Eh! Big danger. Bad water. Push your head right down, drown you dead. And shark, plenty shark."

"Oh, I didn't know that." Melody had seen *Jaws* twice, and she had a healthy respect for sharks. "Thanks for telling me."

"Das okay. You nice lil malihini."

Melody couldn't think of anything else to say, so she went on. That was a nice lady. She hoped they would be friends. Maybe she had some children Melody's age.

She cast a fearful look at the sea as she walked the road to the boat landing. Sharks! She hadn't even thought of that.

It was getting dark inside the cabin when she went back. She found a light switch and flipped it, but nothing happened. She peered up at the overhead light and saw that there was no bulb. There was none in her bedroom either. She considered going to her mother's to borrow a bulb, but decided against it. It was too close to nightfall and she might step on a rat. There were probably scorpions too, and tarantulas.

And her mother might still be mad.

She got into bed with Louella and Bison. "Don't worry," she told them. "It'll be all right. They can't get us as long as we're all together." She propped her stick carefully against the wall near the bed, where she could reach it in a hurry if she needed to.

A sudden shower beat on the tin roof. She heard George come in, heard his exclamation of annoyance when the light didn't go on. Then she saw the beam of a flashlight. George was always prepared for things.

She put the plug of the radio in her ear and flipped the dial. A man speaking pidgin was complaining about the police commission. On another station someone with a high voice that slid from note to note was singing Hawaiian music.

Melody yawned. It had been a long day. She listened, half asleep, to a program called *Island Rock*.

She heard Brian come in, noisy as usual, complaining about the house, about the lack of light, about his mother.

"Edith and her primitive life," he said. "Her in her comfortable apartment. She leaves the primitive life to us."

George said sleepily, "Oh, shut up, Brian."

Melody heard a scuffle, and George said, "Ouch! Cut that out."

In a few minutes Brian began to snore. He had bad tonsils and he always snored. Usually she could sleep through it, the way she had learned to sleep through the sound of jets the winter they lived near the airport, but sometimes it kept her awake.

She fell asleep at last with the sound of an ukulele band in her ear.

6

*S*HE awoke in the pitch dark and couldn't remember where she was. She put out her hand to touch the reassuring silkiness of Bison and Louella's fluffy coat and remembered. She touched her magic stick leaning by her bed. All was well.

For once Brian was not snoring, although she could hear his heavy breathing. If she didn't get so mad at him, she'd feel sorry for him about those tonsils. It must be miserable. In the winter he had one bad cold or strep throat after another. Maybe that was why he got so mean.

The rain had stopped. Faintly she heard music and realized that the radio was still on, the earplug lying on the pillow. She put it in her ear to see if anything was going on that was worth listening to.

". . . and aloha," a pleasant male voice said. "Here we are again, good buddies out there. This is Kahuna the Enchanter, here to spin a few platters and tell a few tales. I've got a nice letter here from Madeline Fujuki. Madeline asks me to play King Kalakaua's song about that little railroad they used to have on Maui. Remember I told you about that song. The King wrote it right after that little railroad made its last run. Used to carry sugar from the plantations to the shipping place. All right, Madeline, here it is and thanks for writing in."

Melody listened. It was a really good song, not a bit like the swoony Hawaiian music they played in California.

"You like that?" Kahuna said, when it was over.

"Yes," Melody murmured, "we liked that." She held Bison and Louella closer so they could hear. The man's voice was very soothing. He had some kind of accent, just a little, but it wasn't pidgin. His voice was gentle and quiet, right inside her head.

"I'll tell you a story now," he said. "You know this one, I bet. All good Hawaiians know this one. But I'll tell it for all you haoles, you Japanese and Korean and Tahitian and Fijan and Marshall Islanders and . . . oh, my, all the wonderful people that make us such a great island."

Melody was getting sleepy, but she managed to stay awake while he told the story of the god Maui, who worried because the sun went across the island so fast, his people couldn't get their planting done. Maui stopped the sun and asked him please to go more slowly so the farmers could plant and harvest.

43

"The sun agreed," Kahuna said, "and ever since we've had nice long days to get things done . . . when it doesn't rain. We can plant the garden, go surfing, fish, and maybe work a little too, right?" He laughed. "I say 'good for you, sun. Thank you, Maui.' All you folks out there, let's hear a thank you for Maui. Okay?"

Melody whispered, "Thank you, sun. Thank you, Maui." She felt sleepy and comfortable. Now she had two friends, the lady who sat on her porch and Kahuna the Enchanter.

In the morning Brian woke her with his usual commotion. He couldn't even brush his teeth quietly. He looked at her, his mouth foamy with toothpaste. He was in his shorts, looking almost as brown as the Hawaiians, his eyes bright blue. He had splashed water all over and thrown a wet towel on the floor.

"Why do you have to make such a mess?" Melody said.

He picked up the wet towel and snapped it at her. It stung her bare legs.

"Stop that. I'll tell."

"So tell, brat. I'm not afraid of Edith." He snapped it again.

"Ow! That hurts."

"That'll teach you not to give me orders."

"I only asked a question. We all have to live in this place. Why can't we keep it neat?" Disorder upset her. Her mother always said, "Melody and George are neat like me. Brian takes after his father."

"I'll live the way I want to," he said. "I'm the oldest."

She knew the dangers of talking back to him, but he made her so angry. "You're messy," she said, "just like your father."

She ducked and ran out of the house. He stood on the steps and yelled at her.

"Stupid! Idiot!"

She picked up a chunk of lava and threw it, but it only bounced off the door that he shut in time.

She went down to the beach. Now she'd have to stay out of the way until he was gone. And she hadn't even washed her face or brushed her teeth.

She scooped up handfuls of seawater and splashed her face. It was warm water, and the salt made her face feel sticky. She waded in up to her knees, keeping watch for water snakes or whatever they were, and watching farther out for any sign of a shark's fin. It seemed strange that such a beautiful place could be dangerous too.

She sat on a ledge of rough lava. Blast that Brian. Some day she'd get even with him. Sometimes she almost felt she could stand up to him, big though he was. She imagined herself staring right into his eyes and casting a spell on him, forcing him to stand still, staring into space, the way people did sometimes in science fiction movies, as if they were frozen in one place. The idea pleased her, and she dabbled her toes in the water, thinking about how long she would keep Brian standing helpless. Right through breakfast, and long enough to make him late for school.

She looked toward the sun. Maui could do a thing like that. Maui had made the sun slow down. She thought about the picture of Maui in one of her mother's brochures—he was big and handsome, and he wore a cape of golden feathers and a tall plumed helmet. She wondered if Kahuna looked like that.

After a while she made a cautious approach to the house and hid behind a tree to see if Brian had gone. Long bell-like blossoms hung from the tree, and the air smelled like flowers.

Brian wouldn't be all that quiet if he were still in the house. She pushed open the door, ready to run if she should be wrong. But the house was empty, the wet towel and Brian's dirty clothes on the floor. She straightened up and emptied the coffee tin he used for his ashtray. She wished he didn't smoke—she hated the smell.

When she had washed up and combed her hair, she hung her clothes on hangers and put them on the pole that ran the length of the house downstairs. It seemed funny to hang your clothes outdoors like that, but it was the only place there was.

On her way to her mother's for breakfast, she passed her friend, the lady on the porch.

The woman waved. "Aloha. How you dis mornin'?"

"Fine, thank you."

The woman was so big, she almost hid her rocking chair, but she was pretty, with dark eyes that smiled.

"How are you?" Melody said politely.

"Fine, fine. Da sun shine for us today."

Melody lingered. "Yes. It's a nice day. Well, good-bye."

"Bye bye. See you bumbye." The rocking chair creaked. "Eh, wait," she called as Melody started up the street. She went into the house and came back with three big papayas. "You like papaya?"

"I love them."

"You take." She held them out. "I got big tree, lotsa papaya. You come when you want, okay?"

Melody felt happy. The sun was shining, she had three papayas and two friends. Tonight she would stay awake and listen to Kahuna the Enchanter. And all day she would roam around the village, and her mother would be too busy to yell at her.

7

ELODY made other friends. She found two Hawaiian girls a little older than she was, who showed her where to find cocoanuts and guavas and wild orchids. They took her fishing in the lagoon and showed her how to catch crabs and how to use small fish as bait for the bigger fish that were good to eat. When she brought home fish for dinner, her mother was pleased. Brian said it wasn't fit to eat, but he wasn't home much anyway. He had made friends with some boys who had motorcycles, and already he was pestering his mother to get him one.

Melody got acquainted with the young minister of the little white church. His name was Mr. Poha, and he told her he was half-Hawaiian, half-Japanese. He had gone to college in Michigan, and he knew a lot of things, like how to hang-glide, which was surprising in a minister.

Melody's mother liked her job, and when she was

happy, she let Melody alone. She played bridge a lot with her tenants, especially a widower from Oregon. She was after him, Brian said, for her fifth husband.

Sometimes she had problems. A couple who smoked pot had to be dealt with because the widower, who lived just above them, was allergic to marijuana smoke. But the situation was solved when the pot smokers swapped apartments with another couple. Sometimes loud parties had to be attended to, and people had to be reminded to put their trash in plastic bags.

Her mother was good at that sort of thing. She could make people do things and still have them liking her. Some of them got a little bugged when she stuck labels on their refrigerators that said, "HAVE YOU TRIED PRAYER?" but they didn't really hold it against her.

Melody overheard a couple talking at the pool.

"Edith is really strung out on religion," the young man said. He was lying on his back on a foam rubber pad beside the pool.

"It's harmless," his wife or his girl said. "No worse than your brother and his Family of Heavenly Bliss."

"Oh, God, not as bad."

The girl noticed Melody then. "Oh, hi," she said. "You came up so quietly I didn't hear you. You're Edith's daughter, aren't you?"

"Yes."

"We really like your mother," the girl said.

"Yes," Melody said. She knew they were afraid Edith would throw them out because they played loud rock late at night.

"Do you always carry that stick?" the man said.

Melody edged away. He might grab the stick. You never knew what people would do.

Her Hawaiian friends, Delia and Chrissy, had noticed her stick, and she had explained to them that it was magic, knowing somehow that they wouldn't laugh. They had been impressed.

"Maybe you're part Hawaiian," Delia had said. "Lots of Hawaiians got magic."

Melody knew both her mother and father had come from Ohio, but she didn't say so. Perhaps after all she was really a changeling. Changelings could be anything.

"You got dark eyes like us," Chrissie said, "and dark hair."

"It won't frizz though. It's straight as a string."

"Maybe she's real magic," Chrissie said to Delia. She giggled. "Maybe she's Madam Pele's sister."

"What was the sister's name?" Melody asked.

"Hiiaka. She was very nice lady."

Okay, she'd be Hiiaka, Melody thought. She did feel a little like Hiiaka."

A few days later she saw Moku again.

"Eh, where'd you go?" he said, flashing his white teeth. "You spose to watch da boat."

"You were gone too long," Melody said. "I had to leave. But I put a good spell on it."

He raised one eyebrow. "Eh! No wonder we catch so many fish."

Melody was impressed. "Did you really?"

"Millions. Some day you come on boat wit' us, I take you for a good ride, okay?"

"I'd love to."

He waved and drove off down the street at top speed.

She told another new friend, Sammy, that she was good luck for fishermen, so he took her fishing and even taught her a little about body surfing. Sammy was a Samoan, younger than she was, but wise in the ways of the sea. He offered to let her try his surfboard, but she was afraid to go out that far because of sharks. She told him her mother wouldn't let her.

She was sorry when the lovely summer days came to an end. School started, and everything changed. The children were bussed to the big school ten miles away. Her friends Chrissy and Delia were in the high school, but Melody was still in intermediate, across the street. She was the only haole in her class. Her teacher was Japanese, Mrs. Kobashigawa, a very nice person but very busy trying to hold onto some kind of order.

Things got into a mess at home. Mr. Smithson, the Oregon widower, moved to Hilo, and for many nights Melody's mother made her children sit and wait for their dinner while she prayed for Mr. Smithson as if he were in mortal danger.

Finally George said, "Edith, in this island there's a tradition of praying people to death."

She looked shocked. "What stupid thing are you saying?"

"If you don't like somebody, you pray him to death. I just thought you might be interested in that interesting fact."

She made him leave the table without his dessert.

Brian started bringing his new friends home to the cabin late at night, and Melody found it hard to sleep. They drank a lot of beer and smoked pot, played their guitars and sang. Sometimes there were girls, and Melody had to turn up the radio loud and wrap her pillow around her head. One night a boy came through the bead curtain in drunken confusion. She jumped out of bed and threatened him with her magic stick. He left.

George moved out and slept at the beach on a hard rock ledge. Melody worried about him because the tide came in so high, but he said his ledge was above high-water mark. Still she worried about him. A picture in the paper one day showed a shark that had foundered in shallow water; some fishermen had hauled him ashore by the tail.

Every night she tried to stay awake for Kahuna's program, or if she was too sleepy, she set her little alarm clock. He seemed like a voice, a friend, inside her skull. He soothed and comforted her with his quiet voice, his music and his stories, especially the stories about Pele, the goddess of the volcano. Some of those stories were pretty scary. There was the one about the quarrel Pele had with her husband, and how to escape her fiery violence he turned himself first into a wild pig, then a stalk of grass, a fern, and at last a tiny fish called a humuhumunukunuku that swam away to safety. Later they made up, and Pele gave him his own volcanoes, Mauna Kea and Kohala, and promised not to cross over into this territory. Since Melody lived near Mauna Kea, she hoped the promise held, but from what she had heard, Madam Pele's track record for keeping her word was none too good.

One day at school a big mean boy named Aaron Kealamakia started shoving her around during recess. He seemed about three times her size, and she was scared. She tried to run but two of Aaron's friends blocked her way. Then out of nowhere came Archie Ah Sing, a small Taiwanese boy who sat behind her in homeroom. He laid Aaron out flat with a Judo throw.

She wanted to thank Archie, but he had already gone, and later he acted as if she didn't exist. During the rest of her classes she worried about how she was going to make it to the bus without getting beaten up by Aaron. She was sure he must be in a rage after being knocked down by a little guy like Archie.

She lingered after the final bell, hoping they would be gone thinking she would take the late bus. When she finally came out, she was sorry she hadn't gone out with everybody else. The playground was almost deserted, except for some boys playing basketball. If Aaron was lying in wait . . .

He was. As she started down the path, she saw him and his buddies come around the corner of the building and start after her. She prayed that Mrs. Kobashigawa or someone, anyone, would come along, but no one did. She forced herself not to run, but panic welled up in her throat as she heard their footsteps close behind her. She wouldn't turn around. She was so tense, she stubbed her toe, and heard their laughter. If she only had her stick! But Mrs. Kobashigawa didn't know, of course, about the magic, and had suggested she leave it home.

The steps behind her were louder, the hard flap-flap of rubber thongs against the paved walk. She began to say in her mind, "I am Hiiaka, sister of Pele. I have magic. No one can harm me." But she wasn't convincing herself at all.

On the sidewalk she stopped to let three big high school boys by. One of them was Lui Nahale-a, a friend of Brian's. All three of them had frizzed-out hairstyles that made their big heads look even bigger.

Behind her Aaron said, "Get her."

She felt a hand grab her shoulder and jerk her backward.

And then something very surprising happened. Lui Nahale-a wheeled around and said something in pidgin so fast she couldn't get it at all, but the hard hand dropped from her shoulder.

"Eh," Lui said to her, "you got pilikia?"

Her mouth was so dry, she could hardly speak. "What?" She was sure he was going to beat up on her, too.

"You got trouble?"

"Kind of," she said.

"My bruddah your friend," he said.

She was thoroughly confused. He must mean *her* brother was *his* friend. "You mean Brian?"

"No, *my* bruddah. Moku."

She couldn't believe it. "Is Moku your brother?"

"He tol' me to look out for you." He took a step toward Aaron Kealamakia, who now looked much smaller than he had before. "You leave lil haole kid alone, you hear? She's my bruddah's friend, you hear dat?"

"Okay," Aaron said meekly.

The two boys with Lui lounged behind him, hands in the torn pockets of their cut-off jeans. The boys with Aaron began to sidle away.

Lui took hold of the front of Aaron's T-shirt. "You unnerstan' me?"

Aaron swallowed. "Sure, Lui. We were just kiddin' around."

"You don' kid around my friend."

"Right, Lui. Sure." As soon as he felt Lui's hand loosen on his shirt, Aaron backed away.

Lui had one eyebrow cocked, and he tilted his bushy head slightly. "You don' forget."

Melody touched Lui's arm. "Lui, tell him not to beat up Archie Ah Sing either. Archie saved me before."

"You hear?" Lui said. "Leave Ah Sing alone, yeh?"

"Yeh, sure, man." Aaron turned and fled.

"Anybody give you any pilikia," Luis said to Melody, "you tell me, yeh?" This time the arched eyebrow and the slight jerk of the head spoke a different message—reassuring, supporting.

"Thanks an awful lot, Lui."

"No sweat." And Lui and his friends slouched off down the street.

8

NE NIGHT when she was listening to Kahuna, he said, "Sometimes I get the feeling there's nobody out there. Just me up here in this studio all alone. Are you out there?"

"We're out here," Melody said. She wished Kahuna could see how quietly Bison and Louella listened.

"Gets lonely around here, midnight to six. That's why I'm happy when you write me letters. Then I know you're there. So keep 'em coming, will you?"

"All right," she murmured. "I'll write tomorrow." She listened to his story about the ohia tree. She was interested because some of the trees on the lane were ohia. Her friend on the porch, Mrs. Kealoha, had told her. The one in front of Mrs. Kealoha's house, which was very big with scarlet blossoms, was supposed to be a thousand years old.

Now Kahuna was telling her that Madam Pele fell

in love with another young man named Ohia. When he said he was sorry but he loved a girl named Lehua and could not marry Pele, Pele got angry and turned him into a tree. The other gods pitied the lovers, so they turned Lehua into scarlet blossoms to hang on the ohia tree. From that day onward Ohia and Lehua were always together.

"Madam Pele tries to get her followers to pick the blossoms and toss them into the crater where she lives," Kahuna said, "but don't do it. When you pick the lehua blossoms, it will rain, and that rain is the tears of all lovers who have been separated. There's a song . . ." He strummed his ukulele a moment and then sang first in Hawaiian, then in English. " 'Pick not the blossom of the great ohia tree . . .' "

"We'll never pick them," Melody said. It was a very sad and beautiful story with a happy ending. It was nice to have a happy ending. She yawned. She couldn't reach the lehua blossoms anyway.

There was a sudden jolt that seemed to tilt the room sideways and back again. Bison fell off the bed. As Melody leaned down to pick him up, the mirror on the wall rattled.

There was a short silence on the radio, and then Kahuna's voice said, "How about that! Madam Pele's mad because I told the ohia story. Did you feel that quake?"

Melody sat up, no longer sleepy. Was Madam Pele

really that real? She was frightened. Pele might hurt Kahuna, if she was angry with him.

Kahuna went on in a different voice. "I haven't got the Richter on it yet. I can't get through to the Observatory. I'll clue you in when I can. It felt to me like about a six on the Richter scale. You folks down near the water, if you're camping out or whatever, I'd move inland if I were you. We might get a tsunami out of that. Repeat: if you're near the water, move away."

"George!" Melody jumped out of bed and ran through the cabin. She had been in Hawaii long enough to know that "tsunami" meant tidal wave. She jumped over Brian, who was sleep on the floor.

George slept with earplugs so the surf wouldn't keep him awake. And if Brian could sleep through the earthquake, George could too. The lava hurt her bare feet as she raced down the road, but she was too worried to be careful where she stepped.

Scrambling down over the rocky ledge, she kept throwing anxious looks toward the black water. Mrs. Kabashigawa had shown them pictures of the devastation after the tsunami that hit Hilo in 1960. The wave had been taller than a high house, and it had smashed everything to pieces for a long way. And in 1976 some campers had drowned in just a small tidal wave.

She tried to run through the knee-deep water

toward George's ledge. The tide was in. When she got to him, he was just starting to stir. He had been lying with his back to the sea, the sleeping bag pulled up around his face against mosquitoes. He sat up and stared at Melody.

"Come quick," she said. "Earthquake."

He didn't wait to ask questions. He jumped off the ledge and waded behind Melody. As they reached the lane, they looked back and saw the water suck his sleeping bag down from the ledge.

He whistled. "Water never came up there before."

"We might get a tidal wave," she said. Her knee was bleeding from a lava cut. "Hurry up." Her wet pajamas stuck to her like Scotch tape.

Brian was just coming out of the cabin, looking sleepy and rumpled.

"Earthquakes," Melody said. "We'd better go to the apartment house."

"Don't tell Edith I lost the sleeping bag," George said in a low voice.

"Of course not."

The three of them ran up the street. Lights were on in the houses, and people were standing around outside. One of Brian's friends yelled at him.

"No sweat, man. Only a five-nine."

"Five-nine what?" Brian muttered. It was always hard for him to make sense when he first woke up.

"Quake," Melody said. "Five-nine on the Richter scale."

Brian veered off to join his friends. There was a light in Mrs. Kealoha's house, and Melody longed to go in. She couldn't think of anyone she'd feel safer with. Even Madam Pele would think twice about harming Mrs. Kealoha.

Her stick. She'd left her stick behind. She stopped in the road.

"What's the matter?" George said.

He would think she was crazy if she mentioned the stick. "Louella and Bison. I forgot them."

"They're all right."

"I can't leave them there. They might drown."

He grabbed her arm to stop her. "You're crazy. Go on to Edith's." He turned and ran back to the lane.

She was touched. She wouldn't have thought George would do that for her. She walked slowly on to her mother's. It was a warm night, with a Kona wind, but she was shivering from the excitement and her wet pajamas. She hoped nobody would notice her.

About a dozen of the tenants were sitting around the pool. Her mother was in their midst, and even before she heard the words, she was sure she was praying.

Melody huddled in a deck chair beyond the area of light and out of her mother's sight. She hoped these people wouldn't laugh at her mother. She watched them.

The young couple who had spoken to her the other

day were off by themselves, whispering and holding hands. Mr. Pepper Wong was checking pipes around the building. Two retired mainland couples, whom her mother often played cards with, sat quietly together with bowed heads. All the others were Japanese. They were quiet, but you couldn't tell what they thought. Nobody seemed panicky, but still, they were out here by the pool at two A.M., and that wasn't exactly normal.

". . . and we put ourselves in your hands, Lord," her mother concluded. "Amen."

Some of the others murmured, "Amen."

"There we are," her mother said brightly, "all shipshape and taken care of."

The young man laughed. "Hey, Edith, you got influence up there, have you?"

Melody tensed. If one of her mother's children had said that, they'd have had their face slapped. But she just smiled and said, "Of course, Peter. The Lord and I have an understanding. As the Hawaiians say, I don't cockroach Him. He don't cockroach me."

Everybody laughed. There weren't any Hawaiians here. Her mother said they couldn't afford the rent. She was rather scornful of Hawaiians.

Mr. Pepper Wong said something to Edith. Melody liked Mr. Wong. He was thin and scholarly-looking, with glasses, tight black silky pants and a smock with a mandarin collar embroidered with blue dragons. He

62

often gave her Chinese cracked seeds, wonderful tasting sticky things. He'd been born in Taiwan.

"Folks, I have an announcement," Edith said, clapping her hands. "Pepper says there's no structural damage. We are a-okay. I *told* you the Lord looks after his children. Has anybody got a radio?"

One of the Japanese men held up a tiny transistor.

"What are they saying, Mr. Yamada?"

"Civil Defense just went off the air. No sign of a tsunami. That second quake was five-nine."

"Well, then, that's fine," Edith said, as if she had personally taken care of it.

"Are your kids okay, Edith?" one of the older men said.

"Oh yes. Pepper went to look. Brian is out on the street with his friends."

And Brian is all that matters, Melody thought.

"Listen," her mother was saying, "since we're all here and wide awake, shall we have a party? I'll make a pot of coffee."

The young couple and two of the Japanese went in to bed, but the others stayed. Melody's mother went to make the coffee, and a Japanese woman went to her apartment to get cookies.

"I'll see if I can dig up a bottle," one of the mainland men said. "This deserves a toast. To Madam Pele." As he walked away, he noticed Melody. "Hey, what have we here?"

His wife said, "Why, it's Melody. Are you all right, dear? You're soaking wet."

"I'm all right." She didn't want to explain. George wasn't supposed to sleep at the beach.

Brian burst in with one of his girls, attracting everyone's attention as usual. "I had to rescue her," he said, his arm around the pretty Filipino girl. "She was scared."

Melody thought the girl looked more embarrassed than scared, but everybody laughed and began to talk to Brian. The popularity boy.

Then George came, with Louella and Bison tucked under his arm. Mr. Poha, the minister, was with him. George slipped behind the azalea bushes, seeking out Melody in her dark corner.

One of the Japanese women noticed the animals and giggled. Brian saw him.

"Hey, there's my baby brother with his cuddly animals." He got a laugh, and sauntered toward George, ready to build the laugh into a big scene. "Folks, do you know any other sixteen-year-old boy, five-feet-ten, all muscle, that's got stuffed animals?"

George turned toward him, lowering his head a little. He reminded Melody of Bison. "Cool it," George said.

Melody got up. She had to save George. "They're my animals," she said.

Brian snatched Bison and held him high, just out of reach. "How much am I offered for this splendid buffalo? The vanishing buffalo."

Mr. Poha said quietly, "Cut it out, Brian."

Melody made a grab for it, but missed.

Brian laughed. "Do I hear ten dollars? Twelve?"

The Japanese woman came back with cookies. She stopped, smiling and puzzled. Everyone watched Brian. He held Bison out over the dark water of the pool. "No bids? Must I destroy this splendid specimen?"

One of the women said uneasily, "Oh, Brian, don't be mean."

"Mrs. Hammond, I'm not mean. Buffalo love water. You've heard of water buffalo? This is a water buffalo."

George made a sudden jump and caught Brian's arm. Bison started to fall toward the pool, but George caught him. Melody was never sure, when she thought about it later, whether George pushed Brian, or whether Brian lost his balance, but he fell backward into the pool with a huge splash.

Melody backed away, clutching both animals, as Brian surfaced, spluttering and furious. Their mother appeared.

"Are we swimming?" she said. "I heard a . . ." She broke off as Brian came up the ladder. "What are you doing in the pool in your clothes? That's not funny, Brian."

Brian tossed back his wet hair. His face was furious. "Tell George. He pushed me in."

Their mother took a threatening step toward George. "Look here," she said.

Melody interrupted. "He didn't push him. Brian tried to throw Bison in, and—"

Her mother interrupted her in a low, angry voice. "Be quiet! Who asked you?"

Melody's voice rose, in spite of herself. "It's not fair. You always blame George. It was Brian that—"

Her mother caught her by the arm in a grip that hurt. "Get out of here. All of you. Get out."

Mrs. Hammond said, "Edith, it was sort of an accident—"

"I don't tolerate rowdies in my family." Then aware that they were all looking at her, she tried to speak more lightly. "Sorry, folks, I'm just not a permissive mother." She gave Melody and George a hard stare. "Leave."

Melody said, "Brian, too?"

Her mother lifted her hand. "Leave! This minute!"

Mr. Poha tried to say something, but she cut him short. "Sorry. That's it. Who's for coffee?"

Melody followed George out to the street. She was sure Brian would be allowed to stay. He'd be forgiven, dried off, fed cookies. It was only with George and her that her mother was not permissive. She said, "George, thanks for getting the animals."

He didn't answer, and she wasn't sure he even heard her. His face was set in a fierce scowl, and he was walking so fast, she had to hurry to keep up with him.

Mr. Poha caught up with them. "Come over to my place. I've got some coffee too."

George hesitated, but Melody wanted to go. She liked Mr. Poha, and she felt uneasy about going back to the cabin. Madam Pele might change her mind and smack them with a big wave yet. This village had been wiped out twice by tidal waves in the last hundred years.

They went into Mr. Poha's pleasant house, and he lit the burner under the coffeepot. Then he found a warm bathrobe for Melody that was several times too big for her. He kept up a cheerful chatter while he made peanut butter and jam sandwiches. Melody sat in a wicker chair with Louella and Bison in her lap, while George leaned against the cinder block wall, silent as he often was.

When Mr. Poha brought in the sandwiches, George said, "She was hitting the bottle."

Melody was startled. They never referred to their mother's drinking except among themselves.

"Yeah," George said, "she was slugging it down when I came in." He had his suffering look. "She'll get smashed in front of everybody."

"You're not supposed to talk about it," Melody said.

"Mr. Poha knows."

Mr. Poha said, "Should I go back?"

"No. That would make it worse. You bug her."

"George!" Melody was shocked.

"It's all right, he knows he does. She doesn't like ministers. She wants to be the whole show. Do all the praying and saving."

"Take it easy, George," Mr. Poha said.

George sat down abruptly on the floor. "Sorry."

"That's all right. Just take it easy."

No one spoke for a few minutes. Melody was afraid she was going to fall asleep. Mr. Poha gave her another sandwich.

". . . and you can't tell me," George was saying, "that it isn't sacrilegious for Edith to stand there telling God where to get off at. Who does she think she is?"

Melody tried to jerk awake and dropped her plate. It shattered on the floor. "Oh! I'm sorry."

"No loss," Mr. Poha said. "It came from Woolworth's." He knelt beside her, picking up the pieces. George got a damp paper towel to wipe up the jam. Melody looked down at the delicate bone structure of Mr. Poha's face and thought, He's beautiful. In a few minutes she was falling asleep again, while Mr. Poha and George talked about God and what religion was. Mr. Poha said there were different forms of faith.

"I believe in Madam Pele," she murmured, but no one heard her. Bison fell to the floor and she scooped him up. "Sit still," she said.

". . . like this Pele stuff," George was saying. Had he heard her after all? "That's just superstition."

"She had a magic stick," Melody said. The scent of

ginger blossoms floated delicately in the room.

"I suppose," Mr. Poha was saying, "myths and legends are symbols of something real. Madam Pele is very real to us because the volcano is always there, a threat. So you get to thinking of it as a person, and the next step is, you propitiate the goddess, try to make her stay cool, not blow her stack. There's some of that in every religion."

"Things have too much power over us," George said. She had never heard him talk so much. "We think we run our own lives, but . . ."

Melody yawned, and her head fell to one side and then jerked up again.

"We have powers of our own," Mr. Poha said. "Faith is power, hope is power, and love is . . ."

Melody fell asleep.

9

EORGE was sleeping in the house again, although when Brian's friends were there, he stayed away until they had gone. Melody saw him one night sitting under the house where the clothes were hung, perched on an old stump, doing his homework by the light of his flashlight.

Brian's parties got pretty rowdy. One morning she told him he was turning into an alcoholic. Disgusted, she kicked at the debris of empty beer cans and cigarette butts.

"Just like your father," she said.

He hit her hard.

When Lui Nahale-a was there, no one bothered her, but sometimes when he wasn't, she had to yell and chase people out of her room. She pulled her bureau across the doorway so at least she'd hear if someone came crashing in when she was asleep.

She slept badly. The pounding of the sea had become a scary sound, and often now there were earth tremors that shook the bed under her. "After-shocks," the radio said. She often woke in panic, feeling that she was being tossed lightly in a blanket, the way her brothers used to toss her when she was little, and that the big throw was about to come. She thought about how the island had been made, in an upward volcanic thrust, and she pictured it sinking again below the surface of the sea without a sound. Each day she checked the little red-bordered box on the front page of the newspaper that reported what was happening inside the volcanoes.

One day in speech class she told one of the stories that Kahuna had spoken of, about the time in 1790 when some warriors who were chasing King Kamehameha and his men got caught in a volcanic eruption. She had looked it up in the library after Kahuna had told the story. It was true, all right, and because she felt the terror of it, she described it with great conviction—the enemy soldiers caught in their tracks by a great upheaval of molten lava, flame, and breath-stopping fumes. She described the glassy black drops of pumice, called "Pele's tears," formed when the molten lava began to harden, and the golden filaments of melted rock stretched out into volcanic glass and called "Pele's hair."

"You can still see the footprints of the men in the lava," she told the class, "after all these years. Some of them have been covered with glass to protect them.

And the way to please Madam Pele, so she won't do this to you, is you take sacrifices and throw them into the pit. You take a piece of pork, some grass, a frond of red fern, and a tiny little fish, because these were the things her husband turned into when he was running away from her." She sat down, feeling a little breathless. She had run over her time, but Mrs. Wang hadn't interrupted her. The class was quiet for a minute or two.

Then a boy said, "How you know? You only a malihini."

She knew "malihini" meant newcomer. There was no way she could answer him, because she *was* a newcomer.

Mrs. Wang was annoyed with the boy. "Me, I'm a malihini too. You think nobody knows anything but you kamaainas?"

A girl named Miranda, a Filipino girl, said, "I thought she did it good. She scared me."

"It scared me too," Mrs. Wang said. "Well done, Melody. Very well done."

Melody was pleased, but later when some of the Hawaiians told her they had liked it, she was even more pleased. The Hawaiians, especially the girls, had left her alone most of the time. It was nice to have them speak to her in a friendly way. But she knew she would never be one of them. It was the first time she had ever been the outsider. Sometimes it made her lonesome, but she tried to forget it by daydreaming about what she'd do when she developed her magic powers. She wouldn't hurt them—they were okay kids—but she'd make them respect her.

That night she finally wrote a letter to Kahuna. She printed it carefully so he wouldn't know she wasn't grown up.

Dear Kahuna the Enchanter:
I listen to you almost every night. Don't get lonesome and feel that nobody listens. I like your songs and stories very much. I feel as if you are talking just to me. Sometimes would you mind playing that railway song again? I really like that.

Yours truly,
Hiiaka, sister of Pele

She put no return address on the letter.

After she had mailed it, she began counting the days till he might refer to it on his program. He was off the air over the weekends. Melody always wished weekends away. Her friends Delia and Chrissy didn't pay much attention to her now that they were all involved in high school. Sometimes Sammy let her go fishing with him, but he usually ended up snorkeling and she didn't have any equipment.

George had a weekend job as a busboy at the Rockefeller hotel. He left early and got back late, riding over with a man who worked in the kitchen.

On weekends he always smelled of food, and Melody liked to imagine broiled mahimahi in herb sauce, sweetbreads, lobster tails.

Their mother had brought Brian a second-hand Honda, on which he roared around the countryside with his friends, making a terrible racket and polluting the air. He had been in trouble several times at school, and on the Tuesday after Melody had written to Kahuna, Brian was suspended for two weeks for smoking pot in the boys' room. His mother was angry with the school authorities, but Brian was pleased because now he could ride his motorcycle all day.

That night Melody set her clock for midnight, to be sure not to miss Kahuna. But he didn't mention her letter. Maybe it was because she hadn't put her real name on it. She huddled under the blanket, trying to protect herself from the mosquitoes. Earlier she had chased an enormous cockroach out of the cabin, and the memory still made her shudder.

She could smell the punk that George kept burning at night outside the cabin to keep off the mosquitoes. It helped some but not enough. Even the evil-smelling stuff she rubbed on her arms and neck didn't stop them. She had written her friend Marg that a Hawaiian mosquito was the size of a jet bomber and had a long lance dipped in poison. The bite didn't just itch, it burned and stabbed.

She sniffed Louella's head. Some of the anti-

74

mosquito guck had gotten on it, and she was afraid poor Louella would go through life smelling terrible.

A sharp wind came up, lifting the fish netting that her mother had put up for "drapes." Now the rain would begin. She started counting to ten, and at eight the downpour came, pounding on the tin roof, rattling the palm fronds like paper. Rain was all right. You could shut yourself up in your mind while it rained. The only thing was, if anything dangerous was happening outside, you wouldn't hear it.

She remembered that her mother, who had been in a good mood all week, had promised to take George and her on a little trip. Wednesday was a no-school day because of teachers' conferences. George wanted to go to the Volcanoes Park, but their mother said they were going to Kalapana, where there was a black sand beach. Melody wasn't so much interested in the black beach, but she was anxious to see the heiau that was just up the road from it. She had read a lot about the heiaus, which were ancient Hawaiian temples, or the remains of them. Kahuna had mentioned the one near Kalapana. An idea was forming in her mind about her stick.

Against her rain-streaked window Melody saw the outline of a gecko. She got up to see if he was inside or out. A gecko was a tiny pale lizard, perfectly made like a miniature dragon. She really liked them. She got as close to the window as she could for a good look, without frightening him away. He arched his tiny neck and looked right at her. He was a lot prettier, had more shape, than the bigger, blobby-looking lizards that seemed unfinished.

"Be careful, gecko," she murmured. "Don't let anything get you." She reached for her stick and made a circle three times in the air around him. "Go safe all your days."

He was gone in a flick of speed that she hardly saw. Back on her bed, she lay still, looking at her stick and praying that nothing would keep her from the heiau.

10

HE ROAD to Kalapana went through Hilo, and their mother insisted on stopping to call Mr. Smithson.

"That's why we're going," George said, when she was in the phone booth. "It's just a trap to hook Smithson." He was glum because he hadn't been able to persuade his mother to go up to the volcanoes.

Melody couldn't think about either Mr. Smithson or the volcanoes. The idea that occupied all of her mind was going to the heiau, near Kalapana Beach, and making her stick officially magic. She had read about that heiau—it was an especially powerful one. If she could just get up there and touch the stones where the sacred fires used to be, that would do it. She was sure of it. It was the most exciting idea she had ever had. The power she would have! The things she would be able to do!

In Melody's opinion Mr. Smithson was a very dull man, but she listened when he told the story of

Kalapana, the man who had come from the island of Kauai to see Pele. Mr. Smithson had a flat midwestern voice, and he told the story in a jokey way, as if it were nonsense. He said Kalapana had longed all his life to see the goddess, and when he finally made it, he was an old man with white hair, which he had sworn not to cut until he saw Pele. But he was so old and frail, he couldn't make the climb to the top of Kilauaea volcano, where Pele lived.

"It was raining buckets," Mr. Smithson said, "typical island weather, so the old boy had to quit and come back down over the pali . . . you know what pali are, don't you? That's Hawaiian gibberish for cliffs. Anyway he prepared to die because he had failed to see Pele. But that night there was a big flash of light in his hut, and there stood this glamorous blonde lady smiling at him. She vanished, but in the morning Kalapana discovered his long white hair had been burned off short."

"Oh, how interesting!" Melody's mother said. "It was Pele herself?"

"You betcha. And after that the old boy was treated with great honor, and when he died, they named the beach after him."

"I think that's fascinating," Edith said. "Isn't that the most interesting story, children!"

George crossed his eyes. But Melody was interested in Pele stories.

"They got a story for everything," Mr. Smithson said. "Primitive people they are, children really. 'Course nobody believes any of that hogwash."

"Oh, of course not," Edith said, but Melody had a feeling her mother might believe some of it. She laughed about these stories, but she couldn't wait to hear them. Melody took a firmer grip on her magic stick.

They came upon Kalapana abruptly, out of cane fields and rather barren country into a sudden vista of lush cocoanut palms fringing the sea. There were cars and campers parked wherever there was an empty space, and a lot of people hung around a hamburger and sushi stand. No one was swimming . . . the DANGER signs were everywhere . . . but out a little way there were half a dozen surfers.

"Stupid island," George muttered. "Every place you go, they've got danger signs."

"You shoulda brought your surfboard, son," Mr. Smithson said, and George didn't tell him that Edith had forbidden him to surf. He did go sometimes, Melody knew, but his mother hadn't found it out yet.

He parked the car, and they went out onto the black sand. It was strange but pretty, the creamy white water curling up on the black beach. Edith unpacked the picnic lunch. She and Mr. Smithson had gin and ginger ale in Dixie cups, and George and Melody had guava juice. It was a good lunch, with lots of sandwiches, potato salad, cold baked fish with some kind of sauce, and a cake. She was a good cook, no doubt about that.

George went off by himself, poking around along the shore. After a while he called Melody to see a manta ray.

She watched the fanlike creature move through the blue-green water. "Are there snakes in the water?"

"No," he said, "but there are moray eels."

"Poisonous?"

"You bet."

She shivered, remembering the one that had shot past her. "Do you want to see the heiau?" She held her breath; she needed George to drive her there.

"Where is it?" He glanced over at Mr. Smithson and Edith, who were sitting close together and laughing.

"Up the road a way. The Chain of Craters road, just before the part that got closed after the lava flow."

"Wander over toward the car. I'll meet you."

When she reached the car, she looked back. Mr. Smithson was taking a picture of Edith with his Instamatic.

George joined her. "I told her I had to get gas."

The entrance to the Volcanoes National Park was a short distance up the road, and in a minute George was pulling into the Park's Wauhala Visitors' Center, where the heiau was supposed to be. Except for a

Park ranger's car, no one was around. They walked up to the open building where there were exhibits of the volcano area and pictures and artifacts of early Hawaiian life.

George put on the earphones that went with the cassette, and he stood listening intently, frowning down at the big bas-relief map as the narrator explained the volcanoes.

Melody left him there. He was a little like their mother, absorbed by facts. She went along the winding path that led up the cliff side. This is a pali, she told herself. A cliff formed by lava flow. It seemed strange that it should be so hard and substantial. There were signs along the way naming trees and flowers, and sometimes briefly describing religious rites. No one was in sight, and the air was very still. She trembled with excitement, but she tried to notice everything.

Some of the signs had verses in both Hawaiian and English. She read part of one aloud: "Here is an offering, O Kane, a pig, a white fowl . . ." Maybe she should have brought an offering, but it was too late now. She had no pig, no white fowl, no uwiwi that swims near the surface, nor any aweoweo that haunts the pool. What pretty things they said, and yet it was very scary.

She came around a corner and caught her breath. There stood the heiau. She had half expected just a pile of long-abandoned rocks, but this was a real place.

Thick lava walls formed a big rectangle, and within the walls were remains of different parts of the temple. She stood looking at it, breathing hard as if she had run uphill. There was a feeling, something in the air, that she couldn't identify.

She looked at the plaque the Park had placed at the entrance. It showed a map of the temple as it had looked before time and weather tore it down. In the far corner there had been a thatched hut. That blackened rock was the place where the sacrifices, often human sacrifices, had been cleansed. On her left was the base of the stone tower where the oracles had been read out. And there, straight ahead of her, so real she could hardly bear to look at it, was the great fireplace where the ritual fires had flamed.

The fires had been built when a sacrifice was required. A man called the mu was assigned to watch and see whom the smoke touched first, for that person would be the sacrificial victim. Even the owner of a boat whose sail was caught in the drifting smoke might become the one to be sacrificed. If the smoke touched no one, the mu himself was the victim.

Melody's hand brushed the rough stone wall, and she jumped back as if she had been shocked. She couldn't remember ever being so frightened, and yet at the same time exhilarated. The stillness and the solitude seemed full of people unseen, the ancient fierce warriors, the screaming victims, the frightened worshippers.

She made herself look at the diagram again. The pile of rocks in the far corner, it said, seemed to be the bone pit, although no remains had been found.

She closed her eyes and was back in the thirteenth century. A war was about to begin. Men in feather caps and plumed helmets, dark men with long spears, men with clubs, thronged around her, and the smell of smoke was acrid in her nostrils. The kahuna hovered in the background, with his power to advise or heal. She saw the fire builders, the priest in the tower, the mu, and the person touched by smoke and dragged to the sacrificial rock. Did he scream?

Her eyes flew open. She wasn't sure she had not screamed herself. "Do what you have to do," she said aloud to herself. And drawing her knees high at each step, she went inside the walls of the temple. A special silence caught her up as if she were in a spell. She walked across the broken lava to the place of the ritual fires. She stopped.

In a loud voice she said, "No. Not me. I am not the victim. I seek magic." She held out her stick and touched it to the blackened rock. Her arm jerked back, and she fled.

She walked along the path rapidly for several minutes, glancing back over her shoulder from time to time, before she realized that she had taken the route away from the Park station. The path wound along the edge of the pali, the sea glittering far below her, like some other world that she might never reach. She looked at the tip of her stick to see if it had turned black, but it looked the same as it always had. She wondered if it would glow in the dark.

She heard a snuffling sound ahead of her. In the silence of the cliff, it sounded loud. Then there was a scrambling noise, and a large boar appeared just above her on the path.

"Oh," she said in relief, "it's only a pig." She stopped and waited for it to get out of her way, but it blocked the narrow passage.

The boar grunted and stamped his foot. He wasn't fat and soft-looking like the pigs she had seen. He was lean and tough and he had two long tusks.

She took a step backward, and the boar advanced, shaking his head and glaring at her. He had long legs with white, almost dainty feet, like an over-weight dancer. His hair was coarse and long.

"Go away," she said. "I'm not going to harm you. I won't turn you into Portuguese sausage. I'm Hiiaka, sister of Pele. I am the kind one."

The boar was moving faster on the downward slope. He snorted again. Melody screamed.

The sound stopped the boar for a moment. Then he lowered his head, and she screamed again. "George!"

She didn't even hear George run up behind her. He yelled at the boar, and grabbing Melody's magic stick, he struck it on the snout. The animal gave a loud, surprised grunt. George hit him again, staying just out of range of the sharp tusks. The boar shook his head and turned back.

"Run!" George grabbed Melody's wrist. As they ran down the slope, he dropped the stick. She pulled loose and picked it up. The boar stood at the rise on the path, watching them.

"Melody! Come *on*. He'll charge."

Clutching the stick she ran after George to the car.

They got in and locked the doors, although the boar hadn't followed them.

"Would he have killed us?" Melody said.

"He might. Anyway he could really hurt. Why did you stop for that stupid stick?"

"It's my magic stick."

George groaned. "Melody, look. A game is a game, but it's time to forget it when your life might be in danger."

"It isn't a game. It was the stick that stopped him."

"Thanks a lot. It was me that stopped him."

"You and the stick. You saved my life. Thank you."

"Melody, magic isn't real. No crazy stick is magic. You've got to start growing up."

"How do you know there isn't any magic?"

"I just know. Everybody knows. It's like Santa Claus."

She thought for a minute. "What was it when Jesus

did that with the loaves and fishes?"

"That's different. That was a miracle."

"Miracles, magic, it's the same difference."

"You'd better talk to Mr. Poha. He can explain." He started the car. "Sticks aren't magic, I know that much."

But she knew he was wrong.

He would never understand. He believed in facts, the kind of things he could touch and see and explain. If Benjamin Franklin had told him about electricity, he probably wouldn't have believed it until he saw that trick with the kite.

"That heiau was something, wasn't it," he said.

"Oh, did you see it?" It startled her, almost as if she thought no one else could see it.

"That's where I was when you yelled. Pretty interesting that people seven hundred years ago knew so much about building things. Especially way out here, where they didn't have other people to learn from. Do you realize these islands are two thousand miles from any other land?"

She realized it. She wasn't too fond of thinking about it.

When they got to the beach, their mother said, "What took you so long?" but she didn't wait for an answer. She was too busy flirting with Mr. Smithson. It made Melody sick. Grown-up people shouldn't act in such a stupid way, holding hands and all that. It was undignified.

On the way back to Hilo there was a lot of snuggling and gin drinking in the back seat, but Melody did her best to ignore it. In Hilo Mr. Smithson did the first sensible thing he had done all day—he took them out for Big Macs and shakes.

Melody kept her eyes closed going home, so she wouldn't be expected to say anything. She felt like a new person, an exalted person, like a knight who has felt the blade of his king on his shoulder. It seemed to her that she must look different.

In bed she talked to Bison and Louella about the day, but not about the heiau. She set her clock for midnight, and came wide awake as she heard Kahuna saying, "I've got a real nice letter here, you folks will never guess who from. Brace yourselves. It's from Madam Pele's sister, Hiiaka. It says so right here—'yours truly, Hiiaka, sister of Pele.' How about that. I am honored. She asks me to play King Kalakaua's song, so here we are, for you, Hiiaka, and if you have the time, say a nice spell for me."

Melody listened gravely. "Isn't that nice," she said to Bison and Louella. "That's just for us." She balanced the stick in her hand thoughtfully. If Kahuna needed her help, she would say a spell for him, but it had come to her that the magic power was a great responsibility and not to be used lightly. Also she wasn't absolutely certain it would work.

11

BRIAN and his friends liked to race their motorcycles up and down the street in the evening. His mother scolded him, but it didn't stop him. The people who lived along the street began to get angry. The noise and the fumes were hard to bear. One night Melody saw a man throw rocks at the boys, but he missed.

Then two chickens were run over, and the owner complained to the police. A big, tough-looking policeman came and had a talk with Edith, and she paid for the chickens.

It was having to pay that angered her the most. All through dinner she complained about her children, although Brian was not there.

"Why pick on us?" George said. "It's not us that kill chickens."

"Don't you worry," his mother said, "when I get my hands on that young man, he'll be sorry. I'm going to take the motorcycle away from him."

But she didn't. He stayed away for two days, and then he and his friends began vrooming through the village again.

It was a Sunday morning. Mr. Poha came out of his church and tried to flag them down, but they ignored him. Melody was in church—she usually went, because she liked what Mr. Poha had to say, and she liked the children's choir, which included her friend Sammy.

Mr. Poha came back into the church looking grim. "There's no point in my trying to preach a sermon today," he said. "We'll sing the closing hymn and call it a day. I'm sorry."

Melody left her back row seat just as the benediction ended. It embarrassed her that her brother had disrupted the service.

"You've got to do something," she said to her mother, but she knew the truth was that there was nothing she could do. Brian was practically a grown man.

In the afternoon, in spite of rain, she went fishing. Chrissy and Delia came along, and she had a good time. It was one of the few times she had been with them since school started. Chrissy let her borrow her snorkel.

On her way home she stopped to give some of her fish to Mrs. Kealoha. Although her friend had not complained, it disturbed Melody that she should be one of those who had to put up with the motorcycles. Mrs. Kealoha gave her some papayas and some guavas and never mentioned Brian.

That evening Brian was gone again, but the village was quiet. George said the fathers of some of the other boys had made them stop riding through town.

When she left for breakfast at her mother's, Brian was asleep. She didn't see him at school. On her way home she waved to Mr. Poha, who was just going into Edith's apartment. She wondered if he was complaining about Brian.

At the cabin Brian was sitting on the steps with his head on his arms. She meant to tell him what she thought of the way he was acting, but when she got close, she saw that his shoulders were shaking. It took her a moment to realize that he was crying. She couldn't remember how long it had been since she had seen him cry.

"What's the matter?" she said.

He shook his head and cried harder. He couldn't hold back the sobs.

She was alarmed. "Did you get hurt or something? Should I get Edith?"

"No," he said in a fierce, strangled voice. "I'd like to kill her."

"What happened?"

"She sold my Honda." He looked up at her. Tears had left dusty little streaks on his face.

"Sold it?"

"Sold it to that stupid haole that lives there with his wife."

Melody had never felt so sorry for him. She knew how she would feel if her mother sold Bison and Louella.

"That jerk," Brian said. He was struggling to stop the tears. "He don't even know how to run it . . . He'll ruin it . . ."

The Honda was the only thing Brian really cared about. "I'll ask her to buy it back."

He sniffed. "When did she ever listen to you?" He wiped his face on his sleeve. Melody went inside and got him a Kleenex. "He'll wreck it. I hope he breaks his neck."

Brian blew his nose and wiped his eyes.

"You want some fried bacon rinds?" Melody said. "I've got half a sack."

"No."

Neither of them heard Lui Nahole-a until he was standing at the foot of the steps. "Brian," he said, "whassa matter?"

"Nuthin'." Brian turned his head away.

Lui sat down beside him and put his big arm around his shoulders. "Whassa matter, bruddah? You been cryin'."

"Tell him," Brian said to Melody.

"Our mother sold his Honda."

Lui looked shocked. "Why she do a terrible t'ing like dat?"

"Because of the racket, I guess," Melody said, "and the chickens. She had to pay." Lui didn't have a motorcycle.

"Stupid chickens," Brian said in a choked voice. "Nothing but skin and bones anyway."

Lui was patting him, big floppy pats on the arm. "Don' worry. We got good time anyway. Moku maybe take us out in his boat. Mo' bettah, eh?"

Brian blew his nose. "He won't take me."

Lui jumped up. "You stay here. Don' go 'way." He ran down the road.

"Moku hates my guts," Brian said. "He won't take me out."

She wanted to say he might because he was her friend, but that wouldn't be what Brian wanted to hear. She wished she could help him. He was a mean brother most of the time, but he was her brother. She knew how the Hawaiians felt about their families—their brothers and sisters and cousins and aunts and uncles. Some of them might be bums or stinkers, but when it came right down to it, they were your own people.

In a few minutes Lui came back looking pleased. "Eh, wash your face and come on. Hele-on, okay?"

"Where?" Brian said.

"Moku and Mr. Poha goin' fishin'. They take us along, but hurry up. Wela ka hao—we have fun, yeh?"

"Mr. Poha's mad at me."

"He say you come. He give you no stink, he promise. Hurry up, man."

Brian went inside and splashed water on his face, and all over the floor. He grabbed his fishing pole and ran off with Lui.

Melody wished she were going fishing on Moku's boat. He'd promised, but he had probably forgotten. She mopped up the water on the floor and then curled up on her bed with Bison and Louella and the fried bacon rinds.

She turned on the radio and heard the tapes of a council meeting. The members were arguing about whether to pay a million dollars to a developer for a beach that they wanted for a public park.

One of the members, who spoke strong Pidgin, said, "Eh, Mr. Chairman, I got somet'ing tell you. I drove up to dat beach las' weekend. Dat beach ain't dere no more."

Somebody said, "What you mean, not dere?"

The man cleared his throat. "All wash out."

There was a long silence. Then the chairman said, "Maybe we better wait, see if it wash in again."

Melody hugged Louella and laughed. Sometimes she loved this island and the Hawaiians so much, she could hardly bear to think of ever leaving. Lui was nice. Moku was nice. Mrs. Kealoha was super. The county councilmen were funny-nice.

"And you're nice," she said to Louella. "And Bison is nice. And sometimes even me, I'm nice."

12

For ALMOST a week Brian didn't show up at his mother's for breakfast or dinner. He came back to the cabin late at night, slept till noon, and was gone again. His mother got notices from the school.

"What can I do if I can't get my hands on him?" she said.

George said he was spending most of his time at his girl's house.

"They'll have the truant officer after him," his mother said.

George shook his head. "I don't think they care all that much. Lots of guys stay out for a while if they want to go fishing or whatever."

One good thing, from Melody's viewpoint, was that George spent more time at the cabin. He had bought two powerful light bulbs, one for the main room, one for Melody's, so they could study "without going blind," as he said. Melody pulled her bed underneath the light.

"I hope Brian feels better," she said, when they were in the cabin that night.

"Why?"

"He felt terrible about the Honda. She shouldn't have shamed him like that."

"Is he supposed to do whatever he wants? Drive everybody up the wall with the noise, kill people's chickens?"

"No, I guess not. Only I felt sorry for him. He might not be as bad as we think."

"Want to bet?"

On a windy Thursday afternoon Melody stopped as she often did to talk to Mrs. Kealoha, who was rocking on her porch, drinking cocoanut milk.

"You want?"

"No, thanks." Melody wasn't all that turned on by cocoanut milk.

Mrs. Kealoha pointed to the palm trees bending in the wind and making a papery rustle. "It be dry weather now. Look how Maui's kite stay in the sky."

Melody smiled. She felt personally fond of the beautiful god Maui, as if he were a friend. She liked to think of him flying his kite.

Mrs. Kealoha finished her cocoanut milk and wiped her mouth. "Pau."

Melody nodded. "Pau" meant finished. She was learning a lot of Hawaiian words at school.

Mrs. Kealoha rocked in her chair. " 'O winds of Hilo, hurry, hurry and come to me.' Dat's Maui's song. You know?"

"No, I don't know that one." The night before, Kahuna had talked to her on the radio again. He had said, "Eh, Maui, what'd you do with my friend Hiiaka? You still out there, Hiiaka? Write to me."

So she had written him again and mailed it on the way to school. She wanted to tell Mrs. Kealoha about it, but she couldn't quite do it. It was another world, a private world where Kahuna sent words out on the air and they ended up in her head, just for her. She never thought about other people hearing him.

"My mother and I are going to Hilo tomorrow after school," she said.

"Hilo nice place. Good ice cream in Hilo."

"Oh, is there?"

"You go dat place down on Kam, near da bay. All kine ice cream." She patted her plump stomach.

Melody had been surprised when her mother had announced that they were going to Hilo. She went fairly often on shopping trips, but she had never taken Melody. But it was true, as she pointed out, that Melody had outgrown her clothes.

Melody had a secret plan to get up early and go over to the radio station to see if she could see Kahuna coming off duty at six. She was sure she would recognize him. She pictured him as looking a little like the pictures of Maui, tall, powerfully built, with a noble dark head. Of course Kahuna wouldn't be wearing a cape of golden feathers or a plumed helmet, but she knew he would look splendid.

When it was time to go to Hilo, Melody's mother made a fuss about her taking the radio. She had already said no to taking Louella and Bison.

"For heaven's sake, Melody, the hotel room will have a radio and a television too."

"I like to listen to my own." Melody couldn't explain about listening to Kahuna late at night. Her mother would never go for that. But it was important to have her radio this time. "Please," she said. "It won't be in the way."

Her mother looked at George. "She even wanted to take those stupid animals. At her age!"

"Oh, let her alone," George said.

She directed her anger toward George. "Could you kindly mind your own business, Mr. Buttinsky? Did I ask you for advice? I said no radio." She held out her hand to take the radio from Melody.

Melody stepped away. "I won't go if I can't take it." It was a risk. She might get left behind, and then there'd be no chance to see Kahuna.

Sometimes, though not often, her mother backed down when Melody spoke up to her. This time she said, "You think it's going to break my heart if you don't go? For all I care, you can wear those worn-out, outgrown jeans till you're arrested."

George laughed.

"At least," Melody's mother said, "get rid of that silly stick. You look like Father Time."

George took the stick. "I'll look after it."

Melody hated to leave it. More and more, she felt incomplete without it. But George would take good care of it. He didn't believe in it, but he knew she did.

When they were in the car, Melody leaned out to wave to George, but he was already walking away, twirling the stick like a baton.

As they drove along, her mother began to fuss about Brian. "He's always with that girl. She's Filipino."

"She's pretty."

"You can't go through life on pretty. That kind of girl hasn't got a brain in her little finger."

Melody giggled. "Nobody has."

"Don't you sass me."

"It was just a joke. But I like Estelita. I think she's good for Brian."

"Oh, so now you know what's good for Brian. A good kick in the right part of the anatomy, that's what's good for Brian."

"He hasn't been so bad lately."

"That's because we never see him. He's always with those people, those Filipinos. Have you seen the shack they live in?"

"Well, we live in a shack, too."

Her mother jammed on the brakes, throwing Melody forward against the dash.

"Ouch," Melody said. "What are we stopping for?"

"We're stopping so I can set you straight. If you keep on arguing and contradicting, I'm going to dump you right here and you can walk home."

Melody knew she meant it. "I'm sorry." And for the rest of the trip, she let her mother talk, and never once said anything more than yes or no. It didn't pay to talk back to her mother.

While she listened with the top of her mind to the litany of woes about the apartment house—the tenants who dumped trash without using a plastic bag, the ones who didn't clean the filter in the laundry, the ones who played the TV late at night—she thought about the chance of seeing Kahuna. Of course he wouldn't recognize her, because he thought she was a grown-up. She wouldn't speak to him, because she didn't want him to know she was just an ugly little haole kid with short straight hair and brown eyes.

She was glad when they came down the high coast and she saw Hilo bay glittering in the sun. Before they reached the city limits, a quick shower drenched them, but it was over in a few minutes. Mrs. Kobashigawa had said that it rained so much in Hilo, if you put all the water together in one year, it would be over twelve feet high.

They checked in at the hotel where they had

stayed when they first came. As soon as they got settled in the room, her mother called Mr. Smithson. Melody got into her swim suit and went down to the pool.

She stayed there a long time, swimming and diving. It was nice to come up through layers of water and see the last faint colors of the rainbow arched across the sky. It rained again, and she swam in the warm rain.

When she finally went back to the room, there was a note and three dollars. "Busy," the note said. "Get some supper. Your Mother." Melody was pleased. Now she could prowl around alone.

She walked over to the shopping mall and bought fried wontons and a loaf of sweet Portuguese bread, then strolled along the waterfront as far as Suisan, the river area where the fishing boats docked and the fish was auctioned off. She hung on the bridge, watching the boats. Maybe tomorrow after she saw Kahuna, she'd come back and see the morning auction.

She came back downtown, found the radio station, and stood looking at it for a minute, though she knew Kahuna wouldn't be there so early. Then she walked a little farther and considered going to a movie, but the marquee showed a Japanese film about karate and a Filipino picture. She bought an ice cream cone on Kamehameha Avenue, so she could tell Mrs. Kealoha about it. It was double-decker, Kona coffee on top of pistachio.

Finally she went back to the room and watched TV. Before she went to bed, she set the alarm clock for five-thirty and put it under her pillow, praying it wouldn't awaken her mother. She went to sleep early so she'd be sure to wake up in time to watch for Kahuna when he came off duty at six. She didn't even hear her mother come in.

13

THE ALARM in her mind woke her a few minutes before the clock would have gone off. In the other bed her mother was sleeping soundly. Melody got up and washed and dressed in silence. She slung the strap of the radio over her arm, and, moving quickly in the gray light, let herself out the door. As a shaft of light from the hall fell across the beds, her mother stirred and turned over. Melody tiptoed quickly down the corridor.

She hoped nobody would ask her where she was going. If someone did, she would say she always went for a walk before breakfast. Sometimes she really did.

The girl at the desk had her back to the lobby.

Outside the entrance a Japanese man was putting newspapers into the case. He smiled at her. "Morning."

The day was coming, silvery light moving up the sky with a touch of pink at the edge. It might rain again, but it would just be a misty warm rain.

She walked to the radio station and checked the Timex watch that her father had given her for Christmas. Her mother said it was cheap, but if he had bought an expensive one, she would have complained about that.

Melody stood across the street from the station, leaning on the window frame of a camera shop. It was five minutes to six.

Two cars went by. A little truck heaped with papayas sped past. An old woman, bent over, wearing a muumuu, wandered along the other side of the street. Thinking of Madam Pele, Melody stepped back into the doorway, but the old woman had no stick, and her skin was dark, not pale like Pele's. Still, Melody watched her out of sight down an alley.

Ten after six. Probably when Kahuna came off the air after all those hours, he would have a cup of coffee and relax a minute. She wondered where he lived and what his real name was. He must have a real name, for voting and getting a driver's license. But to her he would always really be Kahuna, the sorcerer, the enchanter, the man of wisdom.

Twenty past six. Two men parked in the parking lot and went into the station.

At six twenty-five a girl in a purple and blue muumuu, came out, got into a car, and drove away.

At one minutes after six thirty a small, young Oriental man wearing dark-rimmed glasses came out with a briefcase, unlocked a Toyota, and left.

At twenty minutes of seven the ground lurched under Melody's feet. She grabbed at the doorframe to keep from falling. There was a second jolt and she heard breaking glass. Small pieces of masonry fell to the sidewalk. The earth was rocking. The plate glass window of the camera shop cracked diagonally. Melody moved a few steps away. A wooden porch on a house collapsed with hardly a sound.

People appeared, some running, some looking toward the sea. Cars drove away, fast. The severe jolting was over, but the slight rocking motion went on. Melody felt sick to her stomach.

A man yelled at her to get away from the buildings, but she didn't know where to go. She went into the street.

"Earthquake," a woman shouted to her. "Leave."

Leave for where? Where was safe? She was worried about Kahuna. A dozen people had come out of the radio station. He must still be inside. What if it fell down?

Sirens began to wail, a rising and falling sound, eerie and frightening. The wind had died down, and there was a hush, as if everything were holding its breath. Even the water of the bay lay flat and still as a sheet of steel.

The people who had come running out were all gone. She stood in the street, worrying about Kahuna. And her mother. Was her mother all right? Melody had intended to get back before she woke up. She'd be mad.

A Civil Patrol car cruised slowly down the street and stopped. The Hawaiian driver called to her. "Get in. Not safe here."

She got in quickly, bumping her radio against the door.

"Big earthquake," he said. "We get out of here before tsunami comes."

"My mother is at the hotel on the lagoon."

"She'll be okay. They got everybody out of the hotels. You're out early." He smiled at her.

She didn't have to answer, because the two-way radio in the car began to crackle. "Car twelve." The voice gave a long string of orders. "Got that, twelve?"

A tinny voice said, "Got it."

"Car fourteen . . ."

Melody's driver picked up the mike. "Fourteen. Got you."

"Check Banyan Drive. A few hotel people got stranded. Lobby of the Travelodge is flooding."

"Right," the driver said, and made a U-turn.

He drove fast to the arm of the bay where some of the resort hotels were. He picked up three elderly tourists and drove fast toward town again. The tourists were pale and silent.

He glanced at them in his mirror. "You safe. Don' worry."

Melody smiled to herself. He had lapsed into pidgin, although he had spoken to her in standard American. Did they do this sometimes for the tourists?

The man with the aloha shirt and the uncombed white hair said, "How bad was it?"

"Oh, 'bout seven-two."

"Great Scott!" He sounded awed. "The big San Francisco quake was only eight, wasn't it?"

"Eight-two, I t'ink. Depend on where it hit, though, like where epicenter is, y'know? We got epicenter off the coast dis time. Not too much damage, mostly broken glass."

"Might there be a tidal wave?" one of the women said. Her voice quavered.

"Yeah, but you folks be safe where I take you. Evacuation center, high ground, y'know?"

"We just got in last night," the man said. He tried to laugh. "What a welcome."

"Madam Pele, she jus' say aloha," the driver said.

He slowed down, trying to avoid the shattered glass that littered the road. There were no people at all along the bay-front street, but as he drove up the hill away from the water, people stood quietly on the streets in front of their houses, watching the bay. There was no sign of panic, just a quiet watchfulness.

The driver called out to a man in a Civil Defense uniform who was directing traffic away from the downtown area. The man pointed up the road to the school that stood on a rise.

"You be safe here," the driver said, letting them out. "Your mother probably show up here."

But there was no sign of Melody's mother in the groups of people that stood around drinking coffee and talking quietly. A Chinese woman got Melody some cookies and milk from the Civil Defense workers in the cafeteria.

People looked sleepy. One woman was telling the others that she had walked down twelve flights in her apartment building, after the elevator stopped working, only to discover that she had left her car keys in her apartment.

Melody walked over to the playground and looked at the distant bay. What did a tsunami look like? How high did it get? She remembered the pictures of devastation that her teacher had shown the class. She was worried about her mother.

Across the street an elderly Japanese man came out of his house and began to weed his garden as if nothing unusual were happening. Melody noticed that the birds were silent. Only the rise and fall of the sirens broke the stillness. A child standing in the street with a pair of binoculars turned around and looked at Melody through the glasses. It made Melody nervous.

The sky and the sea were gray like the gray of

metal. Far out in the bay the breakwater made a black line across the water. A small boat came into view, cruising along near the shore, unreal in the otherwise motionless scene.

Someone said, "That boat better get out of there."

Someone else said, "It's the Coast Guard."

A tourist said, "We saw a pickup truck upended by the quake. It was in a ditch."

"I wish the darned tidal wave would come," another tourist said. "I don't like this waiting."

Melody turned on her radio and people moved closer to her to hear what was being said. The man who usually did the sportscasts in a fast, excited voice and a strong pidgin accent, was now speaking slowly and calmly, giving instructions to people in the coastal areas to move out. "Anybody that's been overlooked by the Civil Defense or the police, move away from the shore at once. Repeat: move away from the shore. All people in the Keaukaha area, use evacuation route along Baker Avenue. You will be cleared across the air field. People in North Hilo and along the Hamakua coast, proceed to high ground at once. Anyone left on Banyan Drive, leave at once. Anyone in the Kaiko'o Mall area, proceed to one of the evacuation centers."

Melody was frightened. Their hotel was across from the Kaiko'o Mall. Her mother might still be asleep. Except for the moaning sirens, everything was quiet; she might have slept through it all.

Melody started walking down the hill, but the Civil Defense man stopped her. "Don't go that way."

"I've got to find my mother."

"Where's she at?"

She told him the name of the hotel. "She might be asleep or something."

"No way. They got everybody out. She's probably at one of the other evacuation points." He turned to speak to someone else and she tried to slip by him, but his big arm shot out and stopped her.

"No, don't give me no bad time. What's your name?"

"Melody Baxter."

He spoke into his walkie-talkie. "Got a little haole kid looking for her mother. Name's Baxter." He listened for a minute and then said to Melody, "You go sit on the wall. I'll tell you when they find her."

A long-haired boy sitting on the wall said, "Kilauea's going to blow."

"How do you know?"

"She nearly always blows after a big quake."

Melody looked anxiously toward the volcano, far up the road. Don't do it, Madam Pele, she thought, crossing her fingers, please don't do it. If she only had her magic stick . . . She was glad she wasn't up at the heiau. It must be very spooky there now. She thought of the volcano pictures Mrs. Kobashigawa had shown them, fountains of red-hot lava and the wide stream of molten lava pouring down the mountain toward the sea, sometimes toward Hilo.

Someone grabbed her shoulder hard. She was sure it was Madam Pele, but it was not—it was her mother.

"Where have you been?" her mother demanded. "I've been looking high and low. You were gone before it was even light out."

Before Melody could answer, someone said, "Here it comes!"

Melody held her breath, watching the dark line of water that rose silently and swiftly and threw itself against the shore. Even the radio was silent.

"Whew," someone said at last. "That wasn't so bad."

"That's only the first one," someone else said.

The second one was bigger, and the third and fourth came close behind it. Several tall palms wavered and fell very slowly. The fifth wave was the biggest. A small boat broke in half and was washed across the street that parallelled the bay. No one spoke. After a few minutes there was a kind of sigh, as if everyone had let out his breath.

"Looks like that's it," a man said.

It was about fifteen minutes before the Civil Defense man signaled to them that they could leave. Several people jumped into their cars and gunned their engines. A large man in an aloha shirt ran for his car.

Someone said, "That's the guy that owns the men's store on Kam." He laughed. "What you bet it's a good place to pick up some water-stained clothes real cheap."

No one answered him.

"Can we go now?" Melody's mother said to the Civil Defense man.

"Sure. All clear." He smiled at Melody. "I told you you find her."

They had to go along the bay-front road on their way home. People were already collecting to inspect their stores for damage. The depressions in the street were full of water, and dead or dying fish littered the pavement.

"Turn up your radio," Melody's mother said. "I don't trust them, saying it's all okay. What do they know?"

The announcer was saying, ". . . and Madam Pele is letting us off easy this time. The report from Volcanoes Park says there won't be a big eruption. Just a little boil-up." He went on to detail the destruction that the quakes and the tidal waves had caused. Flooded homes and businesses, smashed boats, broken windows, a few small buildings caved in. "There was severe tsunami action on the leeward side. A group of campers got caught on the beach. One adult and two teen-agers drowned, no names released yet. This is Jerry Robbins, one of the campers. He's in the hospital with a broken leg." A boy's voice, sounding stunned, said, "Well, we was cooking breakfast, you know, and . . . we was . . . we hardly felt the quake, but all of a sudden, you know . . ." His voice quavered. ". . . this wave, it come up underneath the holes in the lava, right over us, and I got caught and sucked down and I thought I was going to drown . . . I saw my friend, he got trapped and I don't know if he ever got out . . ." His sob was harsh, and Melody could almost feel it hurting her own chest.

The announcer cut off the tape. "We don't have permission to release the names of the victims yet."

"How do I know where my boys are?" Melody's mother sounded scared. "How do I know what's happened to them?"

Melody had been thinking the same thing, but she said, "They're all right." After all, George had the magic stick.

"Oh, this rotten island," her mother said fiercely.

Melody was startled. "I thought you liked it."

"How can anybody like it? You expect paradise, like they tell you, and what do you get? One disaster right after another."

"I love it," Melody said.

"You would. Just to be contrary."

But it wasn't to be contrary. She did love it. It was her island.

14

OOLS of water stood on the floor of Melody's house, and debris and dead fish were washed up on the porch. A cocoanut palm lay uprooted across the road.

George had moved in with Mr. Poha, and Brian was staying with his girl.

"But Brian's got trouble," George said. "Estelita's got a new boyfriend. He and Brian already had one fight."

"Some Filipino, I suppose," his mother said.

"No, he's Hawaiian. An older guy, through school already. He works in the cane fields. David Ahuna."

"The girl isn't very bright," his mother said, "but she can't be dumb enough to prefer a Hawaiian cane field worker to Brian."

George laughed.

"I know David Ahuna," Melody said. "He's a friend of Moku's."

"Moku," her mother said, "Ahuna. I long for people named Jones and Smith."

"And Smithson," George said. "Did you see Mr. Smithson?"

"Not that it's any of your business, Mr. Wise Guy, but I did. We had a lovely fish dinner."

"I just asked. You don't seem to be in a very good mood."

"Perhaps you don't realize our lives were in danger. I'm supposed to be laughing and singing?"

Melody was thinking about David Ahuna. He paddled on the outrigger canoe team and he looked tough and big, like one of those ancient Hawaiian warriors. Brian better not tangle with David Ahuna.

"Brian better move back where he belongs," their mother said. "First thing we know, he'll be compromised and have to marry that girl."

"People don't get compromised any more," George said. "Anyway I don't think she'd have him."

"Not have Brian? You can't be serious. Melody, you get along and clean up the house. I've got to talk to Pepper about the damage here. I'm afraid to ask."

"It isn't bad," George said. "We cleaned up some broken glass. No pipe damage. The water didn't get up this far." As Melody started to leave, he said, "Your stick is okay, and I've got the animals."

"Oh, thanks." She had been worried when she didn't find them in the house. "Thanks, George."

"And you move back into your own place, George," his mother said.

"No," he said, "Mr. Poha asked me to stay. I'm going to." As his mother began to protest, he said, "You can talk yourself blue in the face, Edith, but I'm staying. He's got a Micronesian kid there, and I'm going to help look after him. His father's disappeared, and his mother's in the hospital."

"How old is he?" Melody said.

"Ten. He's scared. They just came here."

"I will not have you in a home for strays," his mother said.

"Why not? I'm a stray myself." He went out.

Melody worked hard at the depressing job of cleaning up the cabin. She mopped up stagnant water, hung the soggy mats on the outside railing. It was a shuddery job, with drowned cockroaches and big spiders, and in her bedroom a decomposing rat that smelled terrible.

When she had finally brought herself to remove the rat, she went out on the steps to recover. On the radio the sports announcer was back to his normal breezy style.

"Eh, folks, some beeg day, no? How you like them quakes? Seven-two. Lotsa damage. House in Kea-akaha smashed up, lotsa boats bust in, store windows smash. Up at the Park, they say Madam Pele quietin' down now. Somebody musta gone up and geev her some sacrifice, yeh. Well, that's life on the Beeg Island. You know what the bumper sticker say— 'Here today, gone to Maui.' But no kiddin', we love our island, right? Okay, aikane, mo' bettah I give you football scores right now. UCLA beat USC 6–4. Back east, Harvard University beat Brown University, 17–4 . . ."

Melody stopped listening. She went under the house and pulled down her sodden clothes and bundled them up to take to her mother's laundry room. They smelled of mildew.

She was bracing herself to go into the house when George and Mr. Poha came, with the Micronesian boy. Mr. Poha introduced her to the boy.

"Need help?" Mr. Poha said.

She told him about the rat.

He went inside and came back, making a face. "It still smells. Besides, your mattress is soaked. Can you sleep at your mother's?"

"She doesn't have room."

"Then come home with us. The boys can bunk in the living room, and you can have the bedroom."

"I don't want to be in the way," she said

"No way. We need a lady in the house to keep us civilized." He put her wet clothes inside a pillowcase and hoisted it onto his shoulder. "I've got a washing machine, would you believe it? My mother bought it. She thinks I live like a savage."

"Don't tell Edith," George said, "just come."

Melody was grateful. Mr. Poha's house was quiet and clean and pleasant. She liked sitting in a corner with Bison and Louella on her lap and her stick nearby, while George and Mr. Poha discussed life and religion, and the little boy from Micronesia listened with wide, dark eyes and never said a word.

15

Y THE TIME Melody moved back to her own place, Brian had come home too. He had had a bad fight with Estelita, and he was in a foul mood. Melody kept out of his way as much as possible.

At night he had friends in, or he came home late, often drunk and noisy. His mother scolded him, but he yelled at her until she wept. He no longer came to her apartment for breakfast or dinner. Although he had been allowed back into school after his suspension, he got into fights and was threatened with expulsion.

George ate dinner with Mr. Poha, so Melody and her mother had to put up with each other at dinnertime.

On the weekend Melody heard from George that Brian had gone to Estelita's house and made a big scene. Her brothers had driven him off. Melody dreaded his coming home that night. Brian humiliated and frustrated was not someone she wanted to be around.

At midnight he was still not home. She turned on the radio and listened to Kahuna. The night before, he had mentioned her second letter. Tonight he told a story about how Hiiaka, the real Hiiaka, had outwitted a family who charged a toll to cross the bridge over the Wailuku River. "It is better to do without than pay for something that should be free," Hiiaka had said, having destroyed the bridge.

While she was listening, Melody turned on her flashlight and wrote Kahuna another letter. She put it in her jeans pocket to mail the next day, then put out the light quickly as she heard Brian stumbling up the steps with some of his friends. There wouldn't be much sleep tonight.

She heard Moku's brother Lui's voice, and three other boys. She always felt a little safer when Lui was there.

There was a lot of loud talk and laughter and the sound of bottles clinking. Brian began to brag about having stolen David Ahuna's paddle. Melody could tell that the others were not pleased about that. Canoe races were important. Lui tried to make Brian see that he should return it.

"Man, they got a race this weekend."

"Tough," Brian said, "he can paddle with his hands."

In spite of the commotion of the argument, Melody

began to fall asleep. Then Brian burst into her room. She sat up, startled. "What do you want?"

"I want you to take a message to Estelita." He was swaying in the doorway, clutching the beaded curtain around him like a cape.

"Brian, it's almost two A.M." She still had the radio plug in her ear. Kahuna was saying something about Maui.

"So what?" Brian said. "Get up." He came toward her.

"Go away." She felt scared.

"Don't you tell me to go away. Get up."

Lui came in. "Brian, come on."

"This is my house."

"Don't bother Melody, okay?"

Brian made a wild swing at him. "Get up, Melody. I want you to tell Estelita, right now, I got three new girls, three times prettier than she is. Got that?" He pulled off her blanket.

She tried to push him away, but he was too big.

Lui grabbed his arm. Brian made another wide swing at Lui. His arm hit Melody's radio and knocked it to the floor with a crash. The earplug was jerked out of her ear.

Rage hit Melody so hard she could scarcely breathe. "You broke my radio!" She jumped out of bed and grabbed her stick.

Brian stepped back, looking startled. "I didn't mean to . . ."

120

She lifted the stick. "You knocked out Kahuna!"

The Hawaiian boys gathered in the doorway muttered to each other and stepped back. Melody followed Brian into the other room, waving her stick.

"You can't do that to me. I am Hiiaka, sister of Pele." She hardly recognized her own voice. "You smashed my radio, but you can't smash my magic. I have a magic stick." She lifted it high over her head.

Two boys bolted out the door.

"She's crazy," Brian muttered. "She always was."

"I shall pray you to death," Heiika cried in an awful voice. "Beware, beware, beware!" She made three circles in the air with the stick.

Lui and the other boys fled. After a long, baffled stare, Brian stumbled after them. She heard the sound of motorcycles revving up, and the grinding sound of Lui's old car.

She sat down on the nearest chair, feeling as if she had been in a long trance. Louella and Bison were there and she picked them up and held them close. She was scared. "I put a spell on Brian," she said. She picked up the radio and turned up the volume, but there was no sound. "Brian smashed Kahuna." Moving onto her bed, she lay back trembling.

16

BRIAN didn't come back. For the rest of the night Melody kept waking up, listening for him. She wanted to tell him she hadn't meant to cast a spell on him—it was just that she had been so upset when he broke her radio. She would undo the spell when he came back. A person shouldn't cast a spell on her half-brother.

But he didn't come. When George came, sent by their mother to see where Brian was, Melody told him about the radio but not about the spell. He was too practical to believe in spells. He took the radio with him to see if he could fix it.

Later in the day Melody saw one of Brian's friends, but when he saw her, he hastily crossed the street.

In the evening George brought back the radio, fixed. "Just knocked some wires loose." He tried to tell her about resisters and transistors, but she didn't understand all that.

"Mr. Poha says if Brian is mad at you, you'd better come stay with us."

She didn't go, but felt lonelier than usual that night. She went to bed early with the radio, but there was never much she enjoyed until Kahuna came on. The only thing to do was sleep a little, so she could stay awake later.

She stayed awake till almost four o'clock listening to Kahuna, and worrying about Brian. At one point she tried a counter-spell, though it didn't seem likely it would work if he wasn't there. Half-asleep, she staged a three-way argument among herself, Louella, and Bison.

MELODY: What if Brian gets hurt?
BISON: He never gets hurt. He's too tough.
LOUELLA: Nobody's that tough, Bison.
BISON: I am.
MELODY: Wouldn't you shake in your shoes if I cast a spell on you?
BISON: Nah. I'd just stampede and scare you.
LOUELLA: Go to sleep, you guys. Mrs. Kobashigawa will flip if Melody falls asleep in class again.

In the morning a sudden heavy downpour of rain woke her. She lay listening to the rain crashing on the tin roof, as if a paper bag full of water had had a

123

hole punched in it. Today she would mail Kahuna's letter on the way to school. Or maybe wait till tomorrow. She didn't want to be a pest. She yawned. It was Thursday. One more day to go and then she could sleep late for two mornings.

After school that afternoon she saw Brian coming out of the high school grounds. Bison had been right—nothing could hurt Brian. She felt relieved, but also just a little disappointed that her spell hadn't been strong enough.

While she was waiting for the school bus, Moku came by and gave her a ride home. He was happy because he had a new job at the Volcanoes Park.

"What do you do?" She pictured him poking around in Pele's house to see what she was up to.

"Pick up litter. Clean-up man, dat's me. You wouldn' believe, yesterday I count eighty-two beer cans. Not countin' Pepsi, Coke, grape, guava juice, papaya juice, gin bottle. We da drinkin'est people in da world."

"Do you work right around the crater?"

"Sure. Everybody wanna see Madam Pele. They stan' and stare into that crater like they goin' to jump in."

"Does anybody ever jump in?"

He laughed. "Nah."

"I've never been up there."

"Wha'! Never see volcano? Mos' haoles go there first t'ing."

"I saw the heiau, the one near Kalapana."

"Oh, dat's scary. Hey, some day I take you to see Madam Pele, okay?"

"I'd love that."

"You gotta get up early though. I go by your street 'bout six thirty A.M. in the mornin'."

"That's all right. I get up early."

"All right. Some day you ain't got school, you be out on the street and wave me down. Say 'Eh, Moku, take me see Madam Pele'. Okay?"

"Okay. Wonderful. Do you work Saturdays?"

"No. Monday till Friday. Monday is worst. Junk. Hunks of hot dogs, sushi cone, bust-up chopstick, Big Mac box, Primo can, Kirin bottle . . . Madam Pele, she hate a mess."

When he let her off, she ran home and said to Bison and Louella, "You'll never believe where I'm going!"

17

SUNDAY as she was washing up to go to her mother's for dinner, Melody heard someone running. She dried her hands and went to see who it was.

George came up the steps two at a time. He looked pale. "Come to Mr. Poha's right away."

"What's the matter?"

"Brian got hurt. Edith took him to the hospital."

Melody gasped. "Brian."

"He was in a fight with Estelita's boyfriend. Some of the canoe club guys were there, and it turned into a big brawl."

Melody's chest felt so tight, she had trouble breathing. "What happened to Brian? Is he dead?"

"No, of course not. One of the canoe team guys hit him on the head with a paddle. He might have a fractured skull or something."

"He'll die."

"Nobody said that. He's just hurt bad enough to go to the hospital. Mr. Poha took them. He says you come stay with us. Bring your animals."

She got Bison and Louella and reached for her stick, but she jerked her hand back and dropped it.

"Hurry up. Mr. Poha's going to call me if there's any news."

She picked up the stick and followed him.

At Mr. Poha's, she tried to eat the cold pork and bread that George put on the table, but she couldn't think of anything but Brian.

She looked at George sitting tensely by the phone. It was funny, she had always thought he hated Brian. Maybe the Hawaiians were right about brotherhood being so strong a thing. But she had caused this terrible accident to her own half-brother, just because she had lost her temper. She had a dangerous power, and she had used it wickedly. The real Hiiaka would never have cast a deadly spell on her own half-brother. Pele would do it, though. Pele would do it in a minute if she felt like it, because Pele was wicked, and very, very powerful.

Mr. Poha came late that evening. "You two should be in bed," he said. "No, there's no change. The skull is fractured, and Brian is still unconscious. They may have to operate."

Melody began to shake. She held her hands tight together, trying to control them. Mr. Poha got her a glass of warm milk with vanilla and sugar in it.

"Do you think we'd better pray for Brian?" George said.

"It won't do any good," Melody said. "I put a spell on him."

They both looked at her for a moment. Then George said, "She talks like that. She thinks her stick is magic."

"There are different kinds of magic," Mr. Poha said gently. "Maybe if we pray, our magic will offset the bad magic."

George frowned. "You don't believe in that magic stuff, do you?"

Mr. Poha shrugged. "Who knows what magic is?"

"What do you mean?"

"Isn't faith a kind of magic? And love?" He knelt and bowed his head and prayed.

After Melody was in bed, she said Mr. Poha's prayer over in her mind, trying to outdo the power of Pele. But she didn't think it would work. Everybody knew how powerful Pele was. Brian would die, and Melody would have killed him.

Some time later a thought came to her. Pele herself could break the spell. If she went to Pele as Hiiaka, and begged her to cancel the spell, Brian might be all right again. Pele could do almost anything.

She would go in the morning, early, before the surgery happened. She went over in her mind the things she would need to placate Pele: the grass and the fern that grew near the volcano, a piece of pork from Mr. Poha's refrigerator—she could pay him back later—a tiny fish. She would meet Moku when he went to work.

She tried to remember the other things Pele liked. There was the lehua blossom, but she wasn't going to do that, even if she could reach one. The ohelo berries that grew near the summit, if Melody could find the right ones. And a bottle of gin. The owner of the Volcano House used to throw a bottle of gin into the volcano whenever there was an eruption; it said so in one of Edith's brochures. She could sneak a bottle of gin from her mother's kitchen. Her mother never locked her doors.

She set the alarm for five thirty. "You can't go," she told Bison and Louella. "It's too dangerous."

She was up at five, dressing silently in the dark. Taking her stick, she went into the kitchen and got a chunk of Mr. Poha's pork, wrapped it in a sheet of newspaper, and put it in a big paper bag that lay on the counter. Then she found an empty mayonnaise jar, let herself out the back door, and ran down to the sea. It took some wading and splashing around before she caught a minnow to put in the jar. But she finally managed and hurried on to the apartment house.

She didn't dare put on the light, in case someone might see it. Carefully she felt for the cupboard shelf where her mother kept the gin and took down a pint bottle. It was full. Her mother would be furious, but if it saved Brian's life, it would be all right.

Now she had everything. She left the apartment and went to the head of her street to wait for Moku. There was a light in Mrs. Kealoha's house already. Melody stepped into the shadows so she wouldn't be seen.

When she heard Mohu's pickup, she ran into the street.

He was surprised to see her.

"You said you'd take me."

"Sure, sure, I will. But . . . how's your bruddah?"

"That's why I'm going. I want to make a request of Madam Pele."

"Oh, you do, eh? I don't know if she like haoles."

"I can always try."

He didn't laugh. She had known he wouldn't, or she wouldn't have told him. To a Hawaiian, her mission made sense.

"Very bad t'ing dem guys did, bustin' Brian on da head. You could kill a guy with a paddle like that." Then quickly he added, "But Brian'll be okay. He come out of it all right, okay."

They didn't talk much on the long ride to the park. But as they approached the entrance, he said, "Me, I don' get off till three thirty. If you get tired, you want to go home, you go to da Observatory and tell Jake you wanna ride. He come down off the mountain about noon. Very nice guy, a haole from Washington. You tell him you're my friend."

"Okay."

He drove past the Visitors' Center and up the road toward the Observatory. All vegetation seemed to have stopped suddenly, and the land as far as Melody could see was black and jagged, a rolling sea of lava that had hardened.

"Over dere is da caldera. You see in a minute when we get to da Observatory."

"It's scary, isn't it."

"You bet. You can't see it good yet."

She had meant the whole scene was scary.

He pointed to a side road. "You can walk down to the sulphur vents. Steam come up outa rocks and leave yellow crystals. Stinks terrible." He pulled into the Observatory road, a little farther on. "I got to go pick up junk over by the lava tube. Everybody go to look at the lava tube and dump litter. The fern forest, it's pretty but too far for you to walk. You had any breakfast?"

"No." Melody hardly heard him. Over there, just beyond the fence where he had stopped, lay the caldera of Kilauea, the great collapsed top of the mountain.

"Here, take banana. Good for you."

"Thanks a lot, Moku."

"You be careful now. Remember, Jake take you home."

"Sure."

"They got movies at da Visitors' Center, you can see volcano blowing off. Real scary, and free."

At last he went with a squeal of tires. She ran to the fence and made herself look down. It was immense. It made her dizzy to look down into those black depths of twisted lava. On the floor and on the surrounding cliffs continuous clouds of steam spiralled upward. Melody felt chilled, by the sight and by the thin air at the thirty-five-hundred-foot level. She wished she had brought a sweater.

The air smelled of sulphur. How could you be sure it wouldn't erupt while you stood there looking at it? Kilauea sometimes sent up a fountain of lava that was higher than the Empire State Building in New York. In 1950, or maybe it was 1960, that other volcano just behind her, Mauna Loa, had poured out enough lava to make a four-lane highway two-and-a-half times around the world. Melody had memorized the statistics to tell her mother. Now suddenly those figures seemed awfully real.

The crater of Halemaumau lay inside the caldera, some distance away. That was where the lava burst out, and that was where Pele hung her hat. Melody wondered if she could get close enough to it to throw in her gifts.

Absently she ate Moku's banana. She read the signs posted along the rail. The caldera was two miles long by half a mile wide. Remember that for Edith. She paused at the place marked "Wailing Priest Bluff." In

Hawaiian and English it gave the prayer you were to make when you sacrificed to Pele. Carefully Melody learned it by heart.

E Pele E! Here is my sacrifice, a pig.
E Pele E! Here is my gift, a pig.
Here is a pig for you,
O goddess of the burning stones.
Life for me. Life for you.
The flowers of fire wave gently,
Here is your pig. The prayer is done.

She said it aloud, substituting Brian's name in the part that said "Life for me." She hoped the chunk of roast pork would do for a real pig. Poor little pigs, they must have had a hard time when everybody was sacrificing to Pele.

She walked up a slope beyond the railing, to a place where trees and bushes had taken root in the lava. She broke off a frond of the big staghorn fern, pulled up a clump of grass, and put them in her paper bag.

A car drove into the fenced area, and a pair of middle-aged tourists got out, a white-haired man in an aloha shirt, and a woman in a dress of imitation tapa cloth with a puka-shell necklace. The man posed the woman against the background of the caldera and took her picture.

They smiled at Melody. "You're out early too," the man said.

The woman asked her to snap a picture of the two of them.

"Are you here with your family, dear?"

"No," Melody said, squinting into the view finder. "I live here." She closed her eyes and snapped the picture. "Not here, I mean, but down near Hapuna Beach."

"Oh, how interesting. But you're not Polynesian or anything, are you?"

Melody wasn't sure what she meant by "or anything." "I'm from California."

"We're from Rhode Island," the man said. "Biggest little state in the union."

"Let's go get breakfast," his wife said. "This place gives me the creeps."

"We can't go without seeing the crater. It's just a couple of miles up the road."

Melody took a deep breath and said, "Excuse me, could I ride up to the crater with you? I'm . . . uh . . . doing a kind of science project. I think it's a long walk both ways, but I could walk back." She hated asking favors. "Unless you'd rather not."

"Glad to, glad to," the man said. He opened the car door. "Anything for science."

As they drove along Crater Rim Road, Melody politely answered the questions—what was her name, how did she like Hawaii, was it hard to go to school here, did she have brothers and sisters.

They came over the crest of a hill to an area marked

Kau Desert, which seemed even more barren than the area they had already seen. Nothing at all was there except lava and ash.

The man whistled. "Looks like hell froze over."

"Look at all that steam," his wife said in a low voice. "Smell the sulphur. I don't like it, Harry." She pointed to a sign warning people with asthma and lung ailments of the danger. "Harry, it's bad for your asthma. Let's turn back."

"We'll just turn around in that loop up ahead." He turned in at a semi-circle marked Halemaumau Crater. A boardwalk led from the drive to the crater. Melody looked around and realized that they were now actually down inside the caldera.

The woman noticed it too. "Harry, let's go." Her voice was sharp with anxiety.

"All right." He let Melody out. No one was around. "You sure you want to stay here alone? Will you be all right?"

"Oh, sure," Melody said, with more assurance than she felt.

The man began to cough. He waved and drove off. Melody was alone inside the caldera of Kilauea. Alone with Madam Pele.

She walked slowly along the path to the boardwalk. A sign said:

On July 19, 1974, within minutes lava tore from a half-mile fissure in the caldera floor and the cliff top. As a curtain of fire rose skyward, lava advanced along the base of the cliff to bury one fifth of the caldera floor. Two days later the waning fountains died. E Pele E! Your jealousy, your rage, are pacified.

The overcast sky seemed to press down, trapping the great clouds of sulphurous smoke that rose from the clefts in the rock. It was cold. Melody fought back an urge to run from this place. The phrase "within minutes" kept repeating itself in her mind . . . "within minutes lava tore from a half mile fissure . . ."

On the other side of the railed boardwalk, signs read DANGER, followed by Japanese lettering that she supposed said the same thing. She could see no living thing, not even a blade of grass.

She walked up to the solid wooden fence that separated the path from the long drop to the crater and forced herself to look. It seemed as if she were looking all the way into the center of the earth. What kind of goddess would choose such a home?

The sulphur hurt her chest and made her cough. It rose up directly in front of her in clouds, shutting off her view each time and filling the air with an evil smell.

She took the fern from the bag and threw it toward the crater. It disappeared. She closed her eyes and imagined it falling down, down, down, to Pele. She threw the clump of grass, but it caught on the edge of the cliff. She was going to have to step outside the fence to get it. There was no other grass.

Carefully she stepped onto the narrow ledge between the fence and the abyss, inching her way along, holding the paper bag in one hand and the fence in the other. She tried not to look down.

She couldn't reach the grass without letting go of the fence. She held her breath, released her grip on the fence, and reached and stretched until her fingers touched the grass. She pulled it toward her, then found a lava pebble to weight it down and threw it once more. It went over. She took out the jar with the fish. He was still alive, swimming weakly in the salt water. She felt bad about sacrificing the poor little fish.

"I'm sorry," she said, and threw the jar. Somewhere the glass must have struck and shattered, but she heard no sound.

Finally she unwrapped the paper from the pork. "E Pele E! Here is my sacrifice, a pig. E Pele E! Here is my gift, a pig. Here is a pig for you, O goddess of the burning stones. Life for Brian. Life for you. The flowers of fire wave gently. Here is your pig. The prayer is done." She threw it and wiped her hands on her jeans.

Only the bottle of gin remained. She gave it a heave.

"Madam Pele, I have done wrong," she said in a loud clear voice. "I am not fit to call myself Hiiaka, because she was good. I cursed my brother and now he may die. I like to think I am your sister, but I am not. I am only Melody Baxter from San Diego, California. On the mainland," she added, in case Pele didn't know. "I think I have power in my magic stick. I touched it to the source of fire at the heiau, then cursed my brother with it." She coughed as a sulphurous cloud blew into her face. "Please, Madam Pele, undo the curse. You are powerful. You can do it. Please save my brother, Brian." She waited, half expecting some kind of answer. "I think I brought most of what you want. I didn't see any of those berries. And I didn't bring the lehua blossom. I don't think you ought to ask for that. Ohia and Lehua love each other—nobody should separate them."

Realizing suddenly that she was still on the dangerous side of the fence, she pulled herself back. Something wet struck her face. It was snowing! Not fresh, good-smelling snow like the snow in the Sierras, but sodden, discolored, yellowish snow, and its wet mass pressed the sulphur fumes down until it was almost impossible to breathe.

"Pele!" she cried out. "Don't reject my prayer!" She took a step forward, her ankle turned on a jagged piece of lava, and she felt herself falling.

18

FOR SOME TIME she had been conscious of strange sounds and smells; the smells stung her nose like sulphur. She coughed and tried to turn over, but a pain shot through her head. Flinging out an arm to grab lava rock, she hit, not lava rock—something soft and smooth. Like a bed. She opened one eye, although it hurt her head. A face bent over her. Two faces. One of them spoke.

"Feel better, honey?"

She tried to answer, but she didn't know what to say. Better than what?

"I'll get Dr. Chan." That face went away.

She opened both eyes enough to look at the other face. It was the head of a young Oriental man, with dark slanted eyes behind rimmed glasses, and silky hair. He said, "Hello. How do you feel?"

"I don't know." Her wrist felt heavy. She looked at it and saw a splint. "Did I sprain my wrist?"

"You broke it. In two places."

"No kidding." She tried to lift it. It was heavy but it didn't hurt. "Where?"

He pointed to the wrist. "There, and . . ."

"I mean where was I?"

"At the volcano. By Halemaumau."

"Oh." Now she remembered. "Did I fall in? No, if I had, I'd be dead."

"It was close. A Park ranger saw you and brought you in."

"Are you the doctor?" She liked his eyes.

"No, I'm your friend, but I don't know your name."

"How can you be my friend then?"

"I know you as Hiiaka."

She gasped. "How could you?"

"Will you tell me your other name?"

"Nobody knows me as Hiiaka, except . . ."

He nodded. "I am Kahuna."

"No, you aren't."

He smiled. "Honest."

"Kahuna is Hawaiian. He's an enchanter, a medicine man. He looks . . . I think he looks like Maui."

The man gave her a wry smile. "I wish I looked like Maui."

"You're Japanese."

"Korean. But that isn't right for Kahuna either, is it. I'm really sorry to disappoint you."

"I don't believe you're Kahuna."

He closed his eyes and tilted his head, and in the voice she knew as well as her own, he said, " 'Pluck not the lehua from the great ohia tree . . .' "

"You fooled me." She felt as if someone had played a joke on her.

"I didn't mean to. I never knew anyone as young and impressionable as you was listening. Why weren't you asleep at those hours? Anyway, Hiiaka, you fooled me too."

"But you knew I wasn't Hiiaka. Grown-ups don't believe in old goddesses."

"Grown-ups believe in grown-ups. I thought you were a grown-up young lady with a lot of imagination." He smiled, showing his very white teeth. "I was thinking of asking you for a date."

In spite of herself she laughed. "My mother won't let me."

"Who is your mother? The hospital needs to know. All they had to go on was the letter in your pocket that was addressed to me."

"My mother is at the hospital with my brother. What hospital is this?"

"Hilo."

"She's in Kona. My brother got hurt. You better not bother her. That's why I went to the crater, to ask Pele to throw off the spell I cast on him."

"They'll have to let her know you're here."

"No, don't bother her. Tell my brother George. He's at Mr. Poha's, the minister . . ."

There was a commotion in the corridor, and the door burst open. Moku stood there looking frightened.

"Hi, Moku," Melody said. "What's the matter?"

"Whassa matter! Everyt'ing da matter. I ask does my friend take you home. Somebody say lil haole girl almost fall into Halemaumau, gone to hospital. I say to myself, 'Moku, you so stupid! I oughta bus' you in da face, you so stupid, to leave that lil child alone . . .'"

It took Melody a while to convince him that it wasn't his fault. The nurse took him away because she thought he was upsetting Melody. Dr. Chan came and gave her a shot.

When she awoke, a girl was bringing supper, and there was a plumeria lei from Moku hanging from the chair. In the evening George and Mr. Poha came.

"How are you?" George said.

"Fine. I got a slight concussion, and I broke my wrist. In two places."

George groaned. "What timing. What were you doing up there anyway?"

"I went to sacrifice to Pele, to take the curse off Brian."

George looked at Mr. Poha. "My whole family is insane."

Mr. Poha said, "Brian is a little better, Melody. Your mother is going to fly to Los Angeles with him, to see a specialist. Melody, Brian was hurt in a fight. It had nothing to do with you."

But Melody was thinking: Brian is better! Pele did do it after all.

"Brian's father wired the money for the air fare," George said.

The bell rang for the end of visiting hours.

"We'll be in Hilo," Mr. Poha said, "till you can go home."

George said, "Edith gave us to Mr. Poha."

"Gave us?"

Mr. Poha smiled. "I'm going to look after you till your mother gets straightened out and able to cope. Mrs. Kealoha is going to look after the house and cook for us."

"Be sure you get the money," Melody said. "My dad gives money for my support, and so does George's."

"Don't worry. Just get some rest. See you tomorrow."

George lingered. "I brought your radio and the animals. The nurse said you could have them tomorrow."

"That was really nice, George." She looked up at him, thinking how much he had improved. It must be Mr. Poha. Or maybe . . . "I lost my stick up at the volcano."

"I think it's just as well."

143

"Maybe."

"I think you better quit fooling around with that magic bit, Melody."

"All right." But still it did work.

He gave her the little Hawaiian lift of the eyebrow and tilt of the head. "See ya."

"So long, bruddah," she said.

19

$\mathcal{S}$HE had two leis to take home; Moku's and a vanda orchid lei from Kahuna. She enjoyed the drive up the coast. Mr. Poha told them stories about the different kinds of people who had come long ago to work in the sugar cane fields—the Orientals, the Scots, the Norwegians, the Germans . . . His voice made a pleasant hum in her head.

"If you hadn't gone roaring off to the volcanoes in the middle of the night," George said, "you'd have known Brian was better."

"It wasn't the middle of the night. It was six A.M." A thought struck her, and she sat up straight. "What do you mean, I'd have known Brian was better?"

"Edith called us about six thirty to tell us. You were gone already."

Melody frowned. "That can't be."

George turned his head to look at her. "What can't be?"

"It was Pele that made Brian better. But I didn't ask her until after . . ." She broke off, trying to think. George must be mistaken.

"Melody," he said, in an exasperated voice, "will you get it through your head . . ."

"Hold it, George," Mr. Poha said. For a minute he was silent. "Melody, Brian had already regained consciousness before you went to Madam Pele."

"Then she didn't do it?"

"No."

She felt confused. "She could have, though."

"No, Melody, she couldn't. There isn't any 'she'. What there is, is an active and dangerous volcano, and people gave it a name and a personality. We do that sometimes: for instance, the way they name hurricanes on the mainland. But they aren't real people."

"They can kill you."

"Oh yes, you bet they can. But they don't know it. A volcano or a hurricane is a part of nature, and nature has no mind, no consciousness." He paused and added almost under his breath, "At least as far as we know."

"As far as we know." Melody leaned back. "But we don't know all that much, do we." They'd be living with Mr. Poha now, and that would be nice. Was it chance? Or something more?

He smiled. "No, you're right, we don't know all that much."

You see, even he wasn't sure.

"Everybody knows," George said, "that there's no mean old woman stashed away in that volcano."

Neither of them answered him.

That night she was awake and waiting for Kahuna.

"Tonight," he said, "I'm going to tell the story of Princess Kapiolani for my good friend Melody Baxter."

"Hey, listen to that," Melody said to Bison and Louella.

"Kapiolani was the first member of the royal family to believe in Christianity. Her people said she was wrong when she told them that the Christian God was a kind god, not a vengeful one who demanded sacrifice. They told her Pele would be angry if she refused to make the usual offerings. So she said to her people, 'I will prove to you that Pele has no power. I will go to her and defy her.' Her people were very frightened. 'Pele will kill you,' they said. But she went right up to the edge of the crater and said, 'Behold, Pele, I bring no sacrifice. I believe in God the Father and his son Jesus Christ, and they are good. I do not believe in you. Look, Pele, how I eat the berries and give you none. See how I throw away the grass and the amaumau fern. I eat the pork. I bring no lehua blossom. You do not exist. You are a cruel superstition that has kept my people in fear for centuries.' And Kapiolani stood up straight. 'No more, Pele,' she said, and she walked away from Pele's house. The people watching from afar trembled, expecting to see her struck dead. But nothing happened." Kahuna paused. "From that time, the belief in Pele weakened. And that is the true story, Hiiaka, the true story."

"Well," Melody said, "that was very brave. I wouldn't dare to do that. And Kahuna, people do still sacrifice to Pele."

She smiled as Kahuna put on the record of King Kalakauai's train song.

"For my friend Melody. We hope she's feeling a lot better."

Over the sound of the music, a volley of rain pinged off the roof. Against the window she saw the tiny shadow of a gecko. A slight rolling motion rocked the bed, and dishes in the other room rattled.

"About three on the Richter," Melody said. She pulled Bison and Louella under the blankets. "I don't know if God ever really lived in the Islands, but I'll bet he'd find it was pretty surprising." She yawned. "You guys better go to sleep. Before we know it, Mrs. Kealoha will be out there cooking bacon and eggs and slicing up the papayas."

C₀

c.3

Corcoran

Make no sound

DATE DUE

Kueker			
Kueker			

ELEMENTARY SCHOOL
LIBRARY
Rochester, Minnesota